THE EARTH BOOK
OF STORMGATE
One
Poul Anderson

NEW ENGLISH LIBRARY/TIMES MIRROR

To Geoff Kidd

First published in the USA in 1978 by Berkley Publishing Corporation

© 1978 by Poul Anderson

First NEL Paperback Edition July 1980

NEL Books are published by
New English Library Limited from
Barnard's Inn, Holborn,
London EC1N 2JR.
Made and printed in Great Britain by
Hunt Barnard Printing Ltd.,
Aylesbury, Bucks.

45004796 2

ACKNOWLEDGMENTS

These stories were originally published as follows:

'Wings of Victory,' *Analog Science Fiction/Science Fact*, April 1972. Copyright © 1972 by Condé Nast Publications, Inc.

'The Problem of Pain,' *The Magazine of Fantasy and Science Fiction*, February 1973. Copyright © 1973 by Mercury Press, Inc.

'How to be Ethnic in One Easy Lesson' (as 'How to be Ethnic'), *Future Quest*, ed. Roger Elwood, Avon Books, 1974. Copyright © 1974 by Roger Elwood.

'Margin of Profit' (in a different form), *Astounding Science Fiction*, September 1956. Copyright © 1956 by Street and Smith Publications, Inc.

'Esau' (as 'Birthright'), *Analog Science Fiction/Science Fact*, February 1970. Copyright © 1970 by Condé Nast Publications, Inc.

'The Season of Forgiveness,' *Boys' Life*, December 1973. Copyright © 1973 by The Boy Scouts of America.

A CHRONOLOGY OF TECHNIC CIVILIZATION

Note: Although Poul Anderson was consulted during the preparation of this chart, he is not responsible for its dating nor in any way specifically committed to it. Stories are listed by their most recently published titles.

21st C	century of recovery.
22nd C	interstellar exploration, the Breakup, formation of Commonwealth.
2150	'Wings of Victory,' *Analog Science Fiction* (cited as ASF), April, 1972.
23rd C	establishment of Polesotechnic League.
24th C	'The Problem of Pain,' *Fantasy and Science Fiction* (cited as F & SF), February, 1973.
2376	Nicholas van Rijn born.
2400	Council of Hiawatha.
2406	David Falkayn born.
2416	'Margin of Profit,' ASF, September, 1956 (van Rijn).
	'How to Be Ethnic in One Easy Lesson,' in *Future Quest*, ed. Roger Elwood, Avon Books, 1974.
———	'Three-Cornered Wheel,' ASF, October, 1963 (Falkayn).
stories overlap around 2426	'A Sun Invisible,' ASF, April, 1966 (Falkayn).
	War of the Wing-Men, Ace Books, 1958 as 'The Man Who Counts,' ASF, February-April, 1958 (van Rijn). See below: *The Earth Book of Stormgate*.

——— 2427	'Birthright,' ASF, February, 1970 (van Rijn).
	'Hiding Place,' ASF, March, 1961 (van Rijn).
	'Territory,' ASF, June, 1963 (van Rijn).
	'The Trouble Twisters,' as 'Trader Team,' ASF, July–August, 1965 (Falkayn).
	The Trouble Twisters (includes 'The Three-Cornered Wheel,' 'A Sun Invisible' and 'The Trouble Twisters'), Berkley Books, 1966.
2433	'Day of Burning,' as 'Supernova,' ASF, January, 1967.
	'The Master Key,' ASF, July, 1964.
	Trader to the Stars, Berkley Books, 1964.
	('Hiding Place'), Berkley Books.
	('Territory'), Berkley Books.
	('The Master Key'), Berkley Books.
2437	*Satan's World*. Doubleday, 1969, and ASF, May–August, 1968; Berkley Books (van Rijn and Falkayn).
	'A Little Knowledge,' ASF, August, 1971.
	'The Season of Forgiveness,' *Boy's Life*, December, 1973.
2446	'Lodestar,' in *Astounding: The John W. Campbell Memorial Anthology*, ed. Harry Harrison, Random House, 1973 (van Rijn and Falkayn).
2456	*Mirkheim*, G. P. Putnam's Sons, 1977 (van Rijn and Falkayn).
late 25th C	settlement of Avalon.
26th C	'Wingless on Avalon,' *Boy's Life*, July, 1973.
	'Rescue on Avalon,' in *Children of Infinity*, ed. Roger Elwood, Franklin Watts, 1973.
	dissolution of Polesotechnic League.
	The Earth Book of Stormgate (contains 'Wings of Victory,' 'The Problem of Pain,' 'Margin of Profit,' 'How to Be Ethnic in One Easy Lesson,' 'The Man Who Counts,'

'Birthright,' 'Day of Burning,' 'A Little Knowledge,' 'The Season of Forgiveness,' 'Lodestar,' 'Wingless on Avalon,' 'Rescue on Avalon'), G.P. Putnam's/Berkley, 1978.

27th C	the Time of Troubles.

'The Star Plunderer,' *Planet Stories* (cited as PS), September, 1952.

28th C	foundation of Terran Empire, Principate phase begins.

'Sargasso of Lost Starships,' PS, January, 1952.

29th C	*The People of the Wind*. New American Library and ASF, February–April, 1973.
30th C	the Covenant of Alfzar.
3000	Dominic Flandry born.
3019	*Ensign Flandry*. Chilton, 1966. Abridged version in *Amazing* (cited as Amz), October, 1966.
3021	*A Circus of Hells*. New American Library, 1970 (incorporates 'The White King's War,' *Galaxy* (cited as Gal), October, 1969.
3022	Josip succeeds Georgios as Emperor.
3025	*The Rebel Worlds*. New American Library, 1969.
3027	'Outpost of Empire,' *Gal*, December, 1967 (non-Flandry).
3028	*The Day of Their Return*, Doubleday, 1973 (non-Flandry).
3032	'Tiger by the Tail,' PS, January, 1951.
3033	'Honorable Enemies,' *Future Combined with Science Fiction Stories*, May, 1951.
3035	'The Game of Glory,' *Venture*, March, 1958.
3037	'A Message in Secret,' as *Mayday Orbid*. Ace Books, 1961, from short version, 'A Message in Secret,' *Fantastic*, December, 1959.
3038	'A Plague of Masters,' *Fantastic*, December, 1960–January, 1961 as *Earthman, Go Home*. Ace Books, 1961.
3040	'A Handful of Stars,' as *We Claim These Stars!* Ace Books, 1959, from abridged version, 'A Handful of Stars,' *Amz*, June, 1959.

3041	Molitor succeeds Josip as Emperor after brief civil war, supplants short-lived Imperial relative as Emperor.
3042	'Warriors from Nowhere,' as 'Ambassadors of Flesh,' PS, Summer, 1954.
3047	*A Knight of Ghosts and Shadows.* New American Library, 1975 and *IF*, September/October–November/December, 1974.
	/story on Flandry's old age planned/
early 4th millennium	Interregnum.
	Dominate phase.
	Fall of the Terran Empire.
mid-4th millennium	The Long Night.
3600	'A Tragedy of Errors,' *Gal*, February, 1968.
3900	The Night Face. Ace Books, 1978 as *Let the Spacemen Beware!* Ace Books, 1963 from short version 'A Twelvemonth and a Day,' *Fantastic* Universe, January, 1960.
4000	'The Sharing of Flesh,' *Gal*, December, 1968.
7100	'Starfog,' ASF, August, 1967.

THE EARTH BOOK OF STORMGATE

To those who read, good flight.

It is Hloch of the Stormgate Choth who writes, on the peak of Mount Anrovil in the Weathermother. His Wyvan, Tariat son of Lythran and Blawsa, has asked this. Weak though his grip upon the matter be, bloodpride requires he undertake the task.

Judge, O people. The father of Hloch was Ferannian and the mother was Rennhi. They held the country around Spearhead Lake. He was an engineer who was often in Gray, Centauri, and other towns, dealing with humans. They in their turn came often thither, for travel routes crisscrossed above and there was, too, a copper mine not far off. Hloch's parents were guest-free and would house whoever pleased them for days in line, giving these leave to roam and hunt. Moreover, as you well know, because of its nearness to populous Gray, our choth receives more humans into membership than most. Hence we younglings grew up friendly with many of this race and familiar with no few of the winds that blow on their souls.

Rennhi was a quester into the centuries, remembered for her scholarship and for the flame she kindled in those whom she saw fit to teach. High above all, she is remembered for writing *The Sky Book of Stormgate*. In this, as you well know, she traced and described the whole history of our choth. Of the ancestors upon Ythri; of the founders here upon Avalon; of the descendants and their doings unto her own years; of how past and present and future have forever been intermingled and, in living minds, ever begetting each other – of this does her work pursue the truth, and will as long as thought flies over our world.

God stooped upon her before she could begin the next chronicle. Already she had gathered in much that was needful, aided in small compass by her son Hloch. Then came the Terran War, and when it had passed by, ruined landscapes lay underneath skies gone strange. We are still raising our lives anew from the wreckage left by that hurricane. Hloch, who had served in space, afterward found himself upon Imperial planets, member of a merchant crew, as trade was reborn. Thus maychance he gained some further sight across the human species.

So did the Wyvan Tariat think of late, when Hloch had wearied of the void and returned to the winds. His word: 'We have need to grasp the realness of those folk, both those who dwell among us and those who are of the Empire. For this, your mother knew, it is best to fly their ways and see through their eyes – ancestral still more than incarnate, that we may sense what is rising ahead of us in time. Hloch, write the book she did not live to write.'

Therefore, behold these annals, from the Discovery and on through the World-Taking. They are garnered from different trees, and few of them will seem at once to grow toward the same sun. Yet they do, they all do. This is the tale, told afresh, of how Avalon came to settlement and thus our choth to being. This is the tale as told, not by Rennhi and those on whom she drew for the *Sky Book*, but by Terrans, who walk the earth. Hloch will seek to explain what is alien: though only by swinging your mind into that same alienness may you hope to seize the knowledge behind.

Then read.

WINGS OF VICTORY

Our part in the Grand Survey had taken us out beyond the great suns Alpha and Beta Crucis. From Earth we would have been in the constellation Lupus. But Earth was 278 light-years remote, Sol itself long dwindled to invisibility, and stars drew strange pictures across the dark.

After three years we were weary and had suffered losses. Oh, the wonder wasn't gone. How could it ever go – from world after world after world? But we had seen so many, and of those we had walked on, some were beautiful and some were terrible and most were both (even as Earth is) and none were alike and all were mysterious. They blurred together in our minds.

It was still a heart-speeding thing to find another sentient race, actually more than to find another planet colonizable by man. Now Ali Hamid had perished of a poisonous bite a year back, and Manuel Gonsalves had not yet recovered from the skull fracture inflicted by the club of an excited being at our last stop. This made Vaughn Webner our chief xenologist, from whom was to issue trouble.

Not that he, or any of us, wanted it. You learn to gang warily, in a universe not especially designed for you, or you die; there is no third choice. We approached this latest star because every G-type dwarf beckoned us. But we did not establish orbit around its most terrestroid attendant until neutrino analysis had verified that nobody in the system had developed atomic energy. And we exhausted every potentiality of our instruments before we sent down our first robot probe.

The sun was a G9, golden in hue, luminosity half of Sol's.

The world which interested us was close enough in to get about the same irradiation as Earth. It was smaller, surface gravity 0.75, with a thinner and drier atmosphere. However, that air was perfectly breathable by humans, and bodies of water existed which could be called modest oceans. The globe was very lovely where it turned against star-crowded night, blue, tawny, rusty-brown, white-clouded. Two little moons skipped in escort.

Biological samples proved that its life was chemically similar to ours. None of the microorganisms we cultured posed any threat that normal precautions and medications could not handle. Pictures taken at low altitude and on the ground showed woods, lakes, wide plains rolling toward mountains. We were afire to set foot there.

But the natives —

You must remember how new the hyperdrive is, and how immense the cosmos. The organizers of the Grand Survey were too wise to believe that the few neighbor systems we'd learned something about gave knowledge adequate for devising doctrine. Our service had one law, which was its proud motto: 'We come as friends.' Otherwise each crew was free to work out its own procedures. After five years the survivors would meet and compare experiences.

For us aboard the *Olga*, Captain Gray had decided that, whenever possible, sophonts should not be disturbed by preliminary sightings of our machines. We would try to set the probes in uninhabited regions. When we ourselves landed, we would come openly. After all, the shape of a body counts for much less than the shape of the mind within. Thus went our belief.

Naturally, we took in every datum we could from orbit and upper-atmospheric overflights. While not extremely informative under such conditions, our pictures did reveal a few small towns on two continents — clusters of buildings, at least, lacking defensive walls or regular streets — hard by primitive mines. They seemed insignificant against immense and almost unpopulated landscapes. We guessed we could identify a variety of cultures, from Stone Age through Iron. Yet invariably, aside from those petty communities, settlements consisted of one or a few houses standing alone. We found none less than ten kilometers apart; most were more isolated.

'Carnivores, I expect,' Webner said. 'The primitive economies are hunting-fishing-gathering, the advanced economies pastoral. Large areas which look cultivated are probably just to provide fodder; they don't have the layout of proper farms.' He tugged his chin. 'I confess to being puzzled as to how the civilized – well, let's say the "metallurgic" people, at this stage – how they manage it. You need trade, communication, quick exchange of ideas, for that level of technology. And if I read the pictures aright, roads are virtually nonexistent, a few dirt tracks between towns and mines, or to the occasional dock for barges or ships – Confound it, water transportation is insufficient.'

'Pack animals, maybe?' I suggested.

'To slow,' he said. 'You don't get progressive cultures when months must pass before the few individuals capable of originality can hear from each other. The chances are they never will.'

For a moment the pedantry dropped from his manner. 'Well,' he said, 'we'll see,' which is the grandest sentence that any language can own.

We always made initial contact with three, the minimum who could do the job, lest we lose them. This time they were Webner, xenologist; Aram Turekian, pilot; and Yukiko Sachansky, gunner. It was Gray's idea to give women that last assignment. He felt they were better than men at watching and waiting, less likely to open fire in doubtful situations.

The site chosen was in the metallurgic domain, though not a town. Why complicate matters unnecessarily? It was on a rugged upland, thick forest for many kilometers around. Northward the mountainside rose steeply until, above timberline, its crags were crowned by a glacier. Southward it toppled to a great plateau, open country where herds grazed on a reddish analogue of grass or shrubs. Maybe they were domesticated, maybe not. In either case, probably the dwellers did a lot of hunting.

'Would that account for their being so scattered?' Yukiko wondered. 'A big range needed to support each individual?'

'Then they must have a strong territoriality,' Webner said. 'Stand sharp by the guns.'

We were not forbidden to defend ourselves from attack, whether or not blunders of ours had provoked it. Nevertheless the girl winced. Turekian glanced over his shoulder and saw. That, and Webner's tone, made him flush. 'Blow down, Vaughn,' he growled.

Webner's long, gaunt frame stiffened in his seat. Light gleamed off the scalp under his thin hair as he thrust his head toward the pilot. 'What did you say?'

'Stay in your own shop and run it, if you can.'

'Mind your manners. This may be my first time in charge, but I *am* –'

'On the ground. We're aloft yet.'

'Please.' Yukiko reached from her turret and laid a hand on either man's shoulder. 'Please don't quarrel . . . when we're about to meet a whole new history.'

They couldn't refuse her wish. Tool-burdened coverall or no, she remained in her Eurasian petiteness the most desired woman aboard the *Olga*; and still the rest of the girls liked her. Gonsalves' word for her was *simpático*.

The men only quieted on the surface. They were an ill-assorted pair, not enemies – you don't sign on a person who'll allow himself hatred – but unfriends. Webner was the academic type, professor of xenology at the University of Oceania. In youth he'd done excellent field work, especially in the trade-route cultures of Cynthia, and he'd been satisfactory under his superiors. At heart, though, he was a theorist, whom middle age had made dogmatic.

Turekian was the opposite: young, burly, black-bearded, boisterous and roisterous, born in a sealtent on Mars to a life of banging around the available universe. If half his brags were true, he was mankind's boldest adventurer, toughest fighter, and mightiest lover; but I'd found to my profit that he wasn't the poker player he claimed. Withal he was able, affable, helpful, popular – which may have kindled envy in poor self-chilled Webner.

'Okay, sure,' Turekian laughed. 'For you, Yu.' He tossed a kiss in her direction.

16

Webner unbent less easily. 'What did you mean by running my own shop if I can?' he demanded.

'Nothing, nothing,' the girl almost begged.

'Ah, a bit more than nothing,' Turekian said. 'A tiny bit. I just wish you were less convinced your science has the last word on all the possibilities. Things I've seen – '

'I've heard your song before,' Webner scoffed. 'In a jungle on some exotic world you met animals with wheels.'

'Never said that. Hm-m-m . . . make a good yarn, wouldn't it?'

'No. Because it's an absurdity. Simply ask yourself how nourishment would pass from the axle bone to the cells of the disc. In like manner – '

'Yeh, yeh. Quiet, now, please. I've got to conn us down.'

The target waxed fast in the bow screen. A booming of air came faint through the hull plates and vibration shivered flesh. Turekian hated dawdling. Besides, a slow descent might give the autochthons time to become hysterical, with perhaps tragic consequences.

Peering, the humans saw a house on the rim of a canyon at whose bottom a river rushed gray-green. The structure was stone, massive and tile-roofed. Three more buildings joined to define a flagged courtyard. Those were of timber, long and low, topped by blossoming sod. A corral outside the quadrangle held four-footed beasts, and nearby stood a row of what Turekian, pointing, called overgrown birdhouses. A meadow surrounded the ensemble. Elsewhere the woods crowded close.

There was abundant bird or, rather, ornithoid life, flocks strewn across the sky. A pair of especially large creatures hovered above the steading. They veered as the boat descended.

Abruptly, wings exploded from the house. Out of its windows flyers came, a score or better, all sizes from tiny ones which clung to adult backs, up to those which dwarfed the huge extinct condors of Earth. In a gleam of bronze feathers, a storm of wingbeats which pounded through the hull, they rose, and fled, and were lost among the treetops.

The humans landed in a place gone empty.

Hands near sidearms, Webner and Turekian trod forth, looked about, let the planet enter them.

You always undergo that shock of first encounter. Not only does space separate the newfound world from yours; time does, five billion years at least. Often you need minutes before you can truly see the shapes around, they are that alien. Before, the eye has registered them but not the brain.

This was more like home. Yet the strangenesses were uncountable.

Weight: three-fourths of what the ship maintained. An ease, a bounciness in the stride . . . and a subtle kinesthetic adjustment required, sensory more than muscular.

Air: like Earth's at about two kilometers' altitude. (Gravity gradient being less, the density dropoff above sea level went slower.) Crystalline vision, cool flow and murmur of breezes, soughing in the branches and river clangorous down in the canyon. Every odor different, no hint of sun-baked resin or duff, instead a medley of smokinesses and pungencies.

Light: warm gold, making colors richer and shadows deeper than you were really evolved for; a midmorning sun which displayed almost half again the apparent diameter of Earth's, in a sky which was deep blue and had only thin streaks of cloud.

Life: wild flocks, wheeling and crying overhead; lowings and cacklings from the corral; rufous carpet underfoot, springy, suggestive more of moss than grass though not very much of either, starred with exquisite flowers; trees whose leaves were green (from silvery to murky), whose bark (if it was bark) might be black or gray or brown or white, whose forms were little more odd to you than were pine or gingko if you came from oak and beech country, but which were no trees of anywhere on Earth. A swarm of midgelike entomoids went by, and a big coppery-winged 'moth' leisurely feeding on them.

Scenery: superb. Above the forest, peaks shouldered into heaven, the glacier shimmered blue. To the right, canyon walls plunged roseate, ocher-banded, and cragged. But your attention was directed ahead.

The house was of astonishing size. 'A flinking castle,' Turekian exclaimed. An approximate twenty-meter cube, it rose sheer to the peaked roof, built from well-dressed blocks of

18

granite. Windows indicated six stories. They were large openings, equipped with wooden shutters and wrought-iron balconies. The sole door, on ground level, was ponderous. Horns, skulls, and sculptured weapons of the chase – knife, spear, shortsword, blowgun, bow and arrow – ornamented the façade.

The attendant buildings were doubtless barns or sheds. Trophies hung on them too. The beasts in the corral looked, and probably weren't, mammalian. Two species were vaguely reminiscent of horses and oxen, a third of sheep. They were not many, could not be the whole support of the dwellers here. The 'dovecotes' held ornithoids as big as turkeys, which were not penned but were prevented from leaving the area by three hawklike guardians. 'Watchdogs,' Turekian said of those. 'No, watchfalcons.' They swooped about, perturbed at the invasion.

Yukiko's voice came wistful from a receiver behind his ear: 'Can I join you?'

'Stand by the guns,' Webner answered. 'We have yet to meet the owners of this place.'

'Huh?' Turekian said. 'Why, they're gone. Skedaddled when they saw us coming.'

'Timid?' Yukiko asked. 'That doesn't fit with their being eager hunters.'

'On the contrary, I imagine they're pretty scrappy,' Turekian said. 'They jumped to the conclusion we must be hostile, because they wouldn't enter somebody else's land uninvited unless they felt that way. Our powers being unknown, and they having wives and kiddies to worry about, they prudently took off. I expect the fighting males – or whatever they've got – will be back soon.'

'What are you talking about?' Webner inquired.

'Why . . . the locals.' Turekian blinked at him. 'You saw them.'

'Those giant ornithoids? Nonsense.'

'Hoy? They came right out of the house there!'

'Domestic animals.' Webner's hatchet features drew tight. 'I don't deny we confront a puzzle here.'

'We always do,' Yukiko put in softly.

Webner nodded. 'True. However, facts and logic solve puzzles. Let's not complicate our task with pseudoproblems.

Whatever they are, the flyers we saw leave cannot be the sophonts. On a planet as Earthlike as this, aviform intelligence is impossible.'

He straightened. 'I suspect the inhabitants have barricaded themselves,' he finished. 'We'll go closer and make pacific gestures.'

'Which could be misunderstood,' Turekian said dubiously. 'An arrow or javelin can kill you just as dead as a blaster.'

'Cover us, Yukiko,' Webner ordered. 'Follow me, Aram. If you have the nerve.'

He stalked forward, under the eyes of the girl. Turekian cursed and joined him in haste.

They were near the door when a shadow fell over them. They whirled and stared upward. Yukiko's indrawn breath hissed from their receivers.

Aloft hovered one of the great ornithoids. Sunlight struck through its outermost pinions, turning them golden. Otherwise it showed stormcloud-dark. Down the wind stooped a second.

The sight was terrifying. Only later did the humans realize it was magnificent. Those wings spanned six meters. A muzzle full of sharp white fangs gaped before them. Two legs the length and well-nigh the thickness of a man's arms reached crooked talons between them. At their angles grew claws. In thrust after thrust, they hurled the creature at torpedo speed. Air whistled and thundered.

Their guns leaped into the men's hands. 'Don't shoot!' Yukiko's cry came as if from very far away.

The splendid monster was almost upon them. Fire speared from Webner's weapon. At the same instant, the animal braked – a turning of quills, a crack and gust in their faces – and rushed back upward, two meters short of impact.

Turekian's gaze stamped a picture on his brain which he would study over and over and over. The unknown was feathered, surely warm-blooded, but no bird. A keelbone like a ship's prow jutted beneath a strong neck. The head was blunt-nosed, lacked external ears; fantastically, Turekian saw that the predator mouth had lips. Tongue and palate were purple. Two big golden eyes stabbed at him, burned at him. A crest of black-

20

tipped white plumage rose stiffly above, a control surface and protection for the backward-bulging skull. The fan-shaped tail bore the same colors. The body was mahogany, the naked legs and claws yellow.

Webner's shot hit amidst the left-side quills. Smoke streamed after the flameburst. The creature uttered a high-pitched yell, lurched, and threshed in retreat. The damage wasn't permanent, had likely caused no pain, but now that wing was only half-useful.

Turekian thus had time to see three slits in parallel on the body. He had time to think there must be three more on the side. They weirdly resembled gills. As the wings lifted, he saw them drawn wide, a triple yawn; as the downstroke began, he glimpsed them being forced shut.

Then he had cast himself against Webner. 'Drop that, you clotbrain!' he yelled. He seized the xenologist's gun wrist. They wrestled. He forced the fingers apart. Meanwhile the wounded ornithoid struggled back to its companion. They flapped off.

'What're you doing?' Webner grabbed at Turekian.

The pilot pushed him away, brutally hard. He fell. Turekian snatched forth his magnifier.

Treetops cut off his view. He let the instrument drop. 'Too late,' he groaned. 'Thanks to you.'

Webner climbed erect, pale and shaken by rage. 'Have you gone heisenberg?' he gasped. 'I'm your commander!'

'You're maybe fit to command plastic ducks in a bathtub,' Turekian said. 'Firing on a native!'

Webner was too taken aback to reply.

'And you capped it by spoiling my chance for a good look at Number Two. I think I spotted a harness on him, holding what might be a weapon, but I'm not sure.' Turekian spat.

'Aram, Vaughn,' Yukiko pleaded from the boat.

An instant longer, the men bristled and glared. Then Webner drew breath, shrugged, and said in a crackly voice: 'I suppose it's incumbent on me to put things on a reasonable basis, if you're incapable of that.' He paused. 'Behave yourself and I'll excuse your conduct as being due to excitement. Else I'll have to recommend you be relieved from further initial-contact duty.'

'*I* be relieved – ?' Turekian barely checked his fist, and kept it balled. His breath rasped.

'Hadn't you better check the house?' Yukiko asked.

The knowledge that something, anything, might lurk behind yonder walls restored them to a measure of coolness.

Save for livestock, the steading was deserted.

Rather than offend the dwellers by blasting down their barred door, the searchers went through a window on grav units. They found just one or two rooms on each story. Evidently the people valued ample floor space and high ceilings above privacy. Connection up and down was by circular staircases whose short steps seemed at variance with this. Decoration was austere and nonrepresentational. Furniture consisted mainly of benches and tables. Nothing like a bed or an *o-futon* was found. Did the indigenes sleep, if they did, sitting or standing? Quite possibly. Many species can lock the joints of their limbs at will.

Stored food bore out the idea of carnivorousness. Tools, weapons, utensils, fabrics were abundant, well made, neatly put away. They confirmed an Iron Age technology, more or less equivalent to that of Earth's Classical civilization. Exceptions occurred: for example, a few books, seemingly printed from hand-set type. How avidly those pages were ransacked! But the only illustrations were diagrams suitable to a geometry text in one case and a stonemason's manual in another. Did this culture taboo pictures of its members, or had the boat merely chanced on a home which possessed none?

The layout and contents of the house, and of the sheds when these were examined, gave scant clues. Nobody had expected better. Imagine yourself a nonhuman xenologist, visiting Earth before man went into space. What could you deduce from the residences and a few household items belonging to, say, a European, an Eskimo, a Congo pygmy, and a Japanese peasant? You might have wondered if the owners were of the same genus.

In time you could learn more. Turekian doubted that time would be given. He set Webner in a cold fury by his nagging to finish the survey and get back to the boat. At length the chief gave in. 'Not that I don't plan a detailed study, mind you,' he said. Scornfully: 'Still, I suppose we can hold a conference, and I'll try to calm your fears.'

After you had been out, the air in the craft smelled dead and the view in the screens looked dull. Turekian took a pipe from his pocket. 'No,' Webner told him.

'What?' The pilot was bemused.

'I won't have that foul thing in this crowded cabin.'

'I don't mind,' Yukiko said.

'I do,' Webner replied, 'and while we're down, I'm your captain.'

Turekian reddened and obeyed. Discipline in space is steel hard, a matter of survival. A good leader gives it a soft sheath. Yukiko's eyes reproached Webner; her fingers dropped to rest on the pilot's arm. The xenologist saw. His mouth twitched sideways before he pinched it together.

'We're in trouble,' Turekian said. 'The sooner we haul mass out of here, the happier our insurance carriers will be.'

'Nonsense,' Webner snapped. 'If anything, our problem is that we've terrified the dwellers. They may take days to send even a scout.'

'They've already sent two. You had to shoot at them.'

'I shot at a dangerous animal. Didn't you see those talons, those fangs? And a buffet from a wing that big – ignoring the claws on it – could break your neck.'

Webner's gaze sought Yukiko's. He mainly addressed her: 'Granted, they must be domesticated. I suspect they're used in the hunt, flown at game like hawks though working in packs like hounds. Conceivably the pair we encountered were, ah, sicced onto us from afar. But that they themselves are sophonts – out of the question.'

Her murmur was uneven. 'How can you be sure?'

Webner leaned back, bridged his fingers, and grew calmer while he lectured: 'You realize the basic principle. All organisms make biological sense in their particular environments, or they become extinct. Reasoners are no exception – and are, furthermore, descended from nonreasoners which adapted to environments that had never been artificially modified.

23

'On nonterrestroid worlds, they can be quite outré by our standards, since they developed under unearthly conditions. On an essentially terrestroid planet, evolution basically parallels our own because it must. True, you get considerable variation. Like, say, hexapodal vertebrates liberating the forelimbs to grow hands and becoming centauroids, as on Woden. That's because the ancestral chordates were hexapods. On this world, you can see for yourself the higher animals are four-limbed.

A brain capable of designing artifacts such as we observe here is useless without some equivalent of hands. Nature would never produce it. Therefore the inhabitants are bound to be bipeds, however different from us in detail. A foot which must double as a hand, and vice versa, would be too grossly inefficient in either function. Natural selection would weed out any mutants of that tendency, fast, long before intelligence could evolve.

'What do those ornithoids have in the way of hands?' He smiled his tight little smile.

'The claws on their wings?' Yukiko asked shyly.

' 'Fraid not,' Turekian said. 'I got a fair look. They can grasp, sort of, but aren't built for manipulation.'

'You saw how the fledgling uses them to cling to the parent,' Webner stated. 'Perhaps it climbs trees also. Earth has a bird with similar structures, the hoactzin. It loses them in adulthood. Here they may become extra weapons for the mature animal.'

'The feet.' Turekian scowled. 'Two opposable digits flanking three straight ones. Could serve as hands.'

'Then how does the creature get about on the ground?' Webner retorted. 'Can't forge a tool in midair, you know, let alone dig ore and erect stone houses.'

He wagged a finger. 'Another, more fundamental point,' he went on. 'Flyers are too limited in mass. True, the gravity's weaker than on Earth, but air pressure's lower. Thus admissible wing loadings are about the same. The biggest birds that ever lumbered into Terrestrial skies weighed some fifteen kilos. Nothing larger could get aloft. Metabolism simply can't supply the power required. We established aboard ship, from specimens, that local biochemistry is close kin to our type. Hence it is not possible for those ornithoids to outweigh a maximal

24

vulture. They're big, yes, and formidable. Nevertheless, that size has to be mostly feathers, hollow bones – spidery, kitelike skeletons anchoring thin flesh.

'Aram, you hefted several items today, such as a stone pot. Or consider one of the buckets, presumably used to bring water up from the river. What would you say the greatest weight is?'

Turekian scratched in his beard. 'Maybe twenty kilos,' he answered reluctantly.

'There! No flyer could lift that. It was always superstition about eagles stealing lambs or babies. They weren't able to. The ornithoids are similarly handicapped. Who'd make utensils he can't carry?'

'M-m-m,' Turekian growled rather than hummed. Webner pressed the attack:

'The mass of any flyer on a terrestroid planet is insufficient to include a big enough brain for true intelligence. The purely animal functions require virtually all those cells. Birds have at least lightened their burden, permitting a little more brain, by changing jaws to beaks. So have those ornithoids you called "watchfalcons". The big fellows have not.'

He hesitated. 'In fact,' he said slowly, 'I doubt if they can even be considered bright animals. They're likely stupid . . . and vicious. If we're set on again, we need have no compunctions about destroying them.'

'Were you going to?' Yukiko whispered. 'Couldn't he, she, it simply have been coming down for a quick, close look at you – unarmed as a peace gesture?'

'If intelligent, yes,' Webner said. 'If not, as I've proven to be the case, positively no. I saved us some nasty wounds. Perhaps I saved a life.'

'The dwellers might object if we shoot at their property,' Turekian said.

'They need only call off their, ah, dogs. In fact, the attack on us may not have been commanded, may have been brute re-action after panic broke the order of the pack.' Webner rose. 'Are you satisfied? We'll make thorough studies till nightfall, then leave gifts, withdraw, hope for a better reception when we see the indigenes have returned.' A television pickup was customary among diplomatic presents of that kind.

Turekian shook his head. 'Your logic's all right, I suppose. But it don't smell right somehow.'

Webner started for the airlock.

'Me too?' Yukiko requested. 'Please?'

'No,' Turekian said. 'I'd hate for you to be harmed.'

'We're in no danger,' she argued. 'Our sidearms can handle any flyers that may arrive feeling mean. If we plant sensors around, no walking native can come within bowshot before we know. I feel caged.' She aimed her smile at Webner.

The xenologist thawed. 'Why not?' he said. 'I can use a level-headed assistant.' To Turekian: 'Man the boat guns yourself if you wish.'

'Like blazes,' the pilot grumbled, and followed them.

He had to admit the leader knew his business. The former cursory search became a shrewd, efficient examination of object after object, measuring, photographing, commenting continuously into a minirecorder. Yukiko helped. On Survey, everybody must have some knowledge of everybody else's specialty. But Webner needed just one extra person.

'What can I do?' Turekian asked.

'Move an occasional heavy load,' the other man said. 'Keep watch on the forest. Stay out of my way.'

Yukiko was too fascinated by the work to chide him. Turekian rumbled in his throat, stuffed his pipe, and slouched around the grounds alone, blowing furious clouds.

At the corral he gripped a rail and glowered. 'You want feeding,' he decided, went into a barn – unlike the house, its door was not secured – and found a haymow and pitchforks which, despite every strangeness of detail, reminded him of a backwoods colony on Hermes that he'd visited once, temporarily primitive because shipping space was taken by items more urgent than modern agromachines. The farmer had had a daughter . . . He consoled himself with memories while he took out a mess of cinnamon-scented red herbage.

'You!'

Webner leaned from an upstairs window. 'What're you about?' he called.

'Those critters are hungry,' Turekian replied. 'Listen to 'em.'

'How do you know what their requirements are? Or the owners? We're not here to play God, for your information. We're here to learn and, maybe, help. Take that stuff back where you got it.'

Turekian swallowed rage – that Yukiko should have heard his humiliation – and complied. Webner was his captain till he regained the blessed sky.

Sky . . . birds . . . He observed the 'cotes'. The pseudohawks fluttered about, indignant but too small to tackle him. Were the giant ornithoids kept partly as protection against large ground predators? Turekian studied the flock. Its members dozed, waddled, scratched the dirt, fat and placid, obviously long bred to tameness. Both types lacked the gill-like slits he had noticed . . .

A shadow. Turekian glanced aloft, snatched for his magnifier. Half a dozen giants were back. The noon sun flamed on their feathers. They were too high for him to see details.

He flipped the controls on his grav unit and made for the house. Webner and Yukiko were on the fifth floor. Turekian arced through a window. He had no eye, now, for the Spartan grace of the room. 'They've arrived,' he panted. 'We better get in the boat quick.'

Webner stepped onto the balcony. 'No need,' he said. 'I hardly think they'll attack. If they do, we're safer here than crossing the yard.'

'Might be smart to close the shutters,' the girl said.

'And the door to this chamber,' Webner agreed. 'That'll stop them. They'll soon lose patience and wander off – if they attempt anything. Or if they do besiege us, we can shoot our way through them, or at worst relay a call for help via the boat, once *Olga*'s again over our horizon.'

He had re-entered. Turekian took his place on the balcony and squinted upward. More winged shapes had joined the first several; and more came into view each second. They dipped, soared, circled through the wind, which made surf noises in the forest.

Unease crawled along the pilot's spine. 'I don't like this half a bit,' he said. 'They don't act like plain beasts.'

'Conceivably the dwellers plan to use them in an assault,'

27

Webner said. 'If so, we may have to teach the dwellers about the cost of unreasoning hostility.' His tone was less cool than the words, and sweat beaded his countenance.

Sparks in the magnifier field hurt Turekian's eyes. 'I swear they're carrying metal,' he said. 'Listen, if they are intelligent – and out to get us, after you nearly killed one of 'em – the house is no place for us. Let's scramble. We may not have many more minutes.'

'Yes, I believe we'd better, Vaughn,' Yukiko urged. 'We can't risk . . . being forced to burn down conscious beings . . . on their own land.'

Maybe his irritation with the pilot spoke for Webner: 'How often must I explain there is no such risk, yet? Instead, here's a chance to learn. What happens next could give us invaluable clues to understanding the whole ethos. We stay.' To Turekian: 'Forget about that alleged metal. Could be protective collars, I suppose. But take the supercharger off your imagination.'

The other man froze where he stood.

'Aram.' Yukiko seized his arm. He stared beyond her. 'What's wrong?'

He shook himself. 'Supercharger,' he mumbled. 'By God, yes.'

Abruptly, in a bellow: 'We're leaving! This second! They *are* the dwellers, and they've gathered the whole countryside against us!'

'Hold your tongue,' Webner said, 'or I'll charge insubordination.'

Laughter rattled in Turekian's breast, 'Uh-uh. Mutiny.'

He crouched and lunged. His fist rocketed before him. Yukiko's cry joined the thick smack as knuckles hit – not the chin, which is too hazardous, the solar plexus. Air whoofed from Webner. His eyes glazed. He folded over, partly conscious but unable to stand while his diaphragm spasmed. Turekian gathered him in his arms. 'To the boat!' the pilot shouted. 'Hurry, girl!'

His grav unit wouldn't carry two, simply gentled his fall when he leaped from the balcony. He dared not stop to adjust the controls on Webner's. Bearing his chief, he pounded across the flagstones. Yukiko came above. 'Go ahead!' Turekian bawled. 'Get into shelter, for God's sake!'

'Not till you can,' she answered. 'I'll cover you.' He was help-less to prevent her.

The scores above had formed themselves into a vast revolving wheel. It tilted. The first flyer peeled off and roared downward. The rest came after.

Arrows whistled ahead of them. A trumpet sounded. Turekian dodged, zigzag over the meadow. Yukiko's gun clapped. She shot to miss, but belike the flashes put those archers – and, now, spearthrowers – off their aim. Shafts sang wickedly around. One edge grazed Webner's neck. He screamed.

Yukiko darted to open the boat's airlock. While she did, Turekian dropped Webner and straddled him, blaster drawn. The leading flyer hurtled close. Talons of the right foot, which was not a foot at all but a hand, gripped a sword curved like a scimitar. For an instant, Turekian looked squarely into the golden eyes, knew a brave male defending his home, and also shot to miss.

In a brawl of air, the native sheered off. The valve swung wide Yukiko flitted through. Turekian dragged Webner, then stood in the lock chamber till the entry was shut.

Missiles clanged on the hull. None would pierce. Turekian let himself join Webner for a moment of shuddering in each other's embrace, before he went forward to Yukiko and the raising of his vessel.

When you know what to expect, a little, you can lay plans. We next sought the folk of Ythri, as the planet is called by its most advanced culture, a thousand kilometers from the triumph which surely prevailed in the mountains. Approached with patience, caution, and symbolisms appropriate to their psyches, they welcomed us rapturously. Before we left, they'd thought of sufficient inducements to trade that I'm sure they'll have spacecraft of their own in a few generations.

Still, they are as fundamentally territorial as man is funda-mentally sexual, and we'd better bear that in mind.

The reason lies in their evolution. It does for every drive in every animal everywhere. The Ythrian is carnivorous, aside from various sweet fruits. Carnivores require larger regions per individual than herbivores or omnivores do, in spite of the fact

29

that meat has more calories per kilo than most vegetable matter. Consider how each antelope needs a certain amount of space, and how many antelope are needed to maintain a pride of lions. Xenologists have written thousands of papers on the correlations between diet and genotypical personality in sophonts.

I have my doubts about the value of those papers. At least, they missed the possibility of a race like the Ythrians, whose extreme territoriality and individualism – with the consequences to governments, mores, arts, faiths, and souls – come from the extreme appetite of the body.

They mass as high as thirty kilos; yet they can lift an equal weight into the air or, unhampered, fly like demons. Hence they maintain civilization without the need to crowd together in cities. Their townspeople are mostly wing-clipped criminals and slaves. Today their wiser heads hope robots will end the need for that.

Hands? The original talons, modified for manipulating. Feet? Those claws on the wings, a juvenile feature which persisted and developed, just as man's large head and sparse hair derive from the juvenile or fetal ape. The forepart of the wing skeleton consists of humerus, radius, and ulnar, much as in true birds. These lock together in flight. Aground, when the wing is folded downward, they produce a 'knee' joint. Bones grow from their base to make the claw-foot. Three fused digits, immensely lengthened, sweep backward to be the alatan which braces the rest of that tremendous wing and can, when desired, give additional support on the surface. To rise, the Ythrians usually do a handstand during the initial upstroke. It takes less than a second.

Oh, yes, they are slow and awkward afoot. They manage, though. Big and beweaponed, instantly ready to mount the wind, they need fear no beast of prey.

You ask where the power comes from to swing this hugeness through the sky. The oxidation of food, what else? Hence the demand of each household for a great hunting or ranching demesne. The limiting factor is the oxygen supply. A molecule in the blood can carry more than hemoglobin does, but the gas must be furnished. Turekian first realized how that happens.

The Ythrian has lungs, a passive system resembling ours. In addition he has his supercharger, evolved from the gills of an amphibianlike ancestor. Worked in bellows fashion by the flight muscles, connecting directly with the bloodstream, those air-intake organs let him burn his fuel as fast as necessary.

I wonder how it feels to be so alive.

I remember how Yukiko Sachansky stood in the curve of Aram Turekian's arm, under a dawn heaven, and watched the farewell dance the Ythrians gave for us, and cried through tears: 'To fly like that! To fly like that!'

This happened early in the course of starflight. The tale is in *Far Adventure* by Maeve Downey, the autobiography of a planetologist. Aside from scientific reports which the same expedition rendered, it appears to be the first outside account of us.

You well know how the Discovery gale-seized those peoples who had the learning to see what it meant, so that erelong all Ythri could never again speak in full understanding, through books and songs and art, with the ancestors. The dealings with Terrans as these returned, first for study and later for trade; the quest and strife which slowly won for us our own modern technics; the passion of history through life after life: these are in many writings. What is less known than it should be is how the Terrans themselves were faring meanwhile.

Their Commonwealth had been formed out of numerous *nations*. A few more came into being and membership afterward. To explain the concept 'nation' is stiffly upwind. As a snatching at the task – Within a sharply defined territory dwell a large number of humans who, in a subtle sense which goes beyond private property or shared range, identify their souls with this land and with each other. Law and mutual obligation are maintained less by usage and pride than by physical violence or the threat thereof on the part of that institution called the government. It is as if a single group could permanently cry Oherran against the entire rest of society, bring death and devastation wherever it chose, and claimed this as an exclusive right. Compliance and assistance are said to be honorable, resistance dishonorable, especially when one nation is at war with another – for each of these entities has powers which are limited not by justice, decency, or prudence, but only by its own strength.

You well know how most humans on Avalon still maintain a modified form of government. However, this is of sharply limited force, both in practice and in law. It is merely their way. You cannot mind-grasp the modern Terran Empire without knowing what a nation truly is.

To curb these inordinate prerogatives of a few, whose quarrels and mismanagement threatened to lay waste their native planet, the Commonwealth was finally established, as a nation of nations. This did not happen quickly, easily, or rationally. The story of it is long and terrible. Nevertheless, it happened: and, for a time, the Commonwealth was on the whole a benign influence. Under its protection, both prosperity and freedom from demands flourished ever more greatly.

Meanwhile exploration exploded throughout this part of the galaxy. Human-habitable worlds which had no intelligent life of their own began to be settled. Our species, in slow youngling wise, began to venture from its nest, at first usually in a flock with Terrans.

The same expedition which made the Discovery of Ythri had chanced upon Avalon. Though rich prey for colonists, at the time it lay too far from Sol and remained nameless. The season came at last for taking real knowledge of it. Because Ythrians were also a-wing in this, there happened an incident which is worth the telling here. Rennhi found the account, transcribed from a recording made on Terra, in the archives of the University of Fleurville upon the planet Esperance. It was originally part of a private correspondence between two humans, preserved by the heirs of the recipient after his death; a visiting historian obtained a copy but never published it. God hunted down all persons concerned so long ago that no pride will be touched by planting the story here.

The value of it lies in the human look upon us, a look which tried to reach down into the spirit and thereby, maychance, now opens for us a glimpse into theirs.

THE PROBLEM OF PAIN

Maybe only a Christian can understand this story. In that case I don't qualify. But I do take an interest in religion, as part of being an amateur psychologist, and – for the grandeur of its language if nothing else – a Bible is among the reels that accompany me wherever I go. This was one reason Peter Berg told me what had happened in his past. He desperately needed to make sense of it, and no priest he'd talked to had quite laid his questions to rest. There was an outside chance that an outside viewpoint like mine would see what a man within the faith couldn't.

His other reason was simple loneliness. We were on Lucifer, as part of a study corporation. That world is well named. It will never be a real colony for any beings whose ancestors evolved amidst clean greenery. But it might be marginally habitable, and if so, its mineral wealth would be worth exploiting. Our job was to determine whether that was true. The gentlest-looking environment holds a thousand death traps until you have learned what the difficulties are and how to grip them. (Earth is no exception.) Sometimes you find problems which can't be solved economically, or can't be solved at all. Then you write off the area or the entire planet, and look for another.

We'd contracted to work three standard years on Lucifer. The pay was munificent, but presently we realized that no bank account could buy back one day we might have spent beneath a kindlier sun. It was a knowledge we carefully avoided discussing with teammates.

About midway through, Peter Berg and I were assigned to do an in-depth investigation of a unique cycle in the ecology of the northern middle latitudes. This meant that we settled down for weeks – which ran into months – in a sample region, well away from everybody else to minimize human disturbances. An occasional supply flitter gave us our only real contact; electronics were no proper substitute, especially when that hell-violent star was forever disrupting them.

Under such circumstances, you come to know your partner maybe better than you know yourself. Pete and I got along well. He's a big, sandy-haired, freckle-faced young man, altogether dependable, with enough kindliness, courtesy, and dignity that he need not make a show of them. Soft-spoken, he's a bit short in the humor department. Otherwise I recommend him as a companion. He has a lot to tell from his own wanderings, yet he'll listen with genuine interest to your memories and brags; he's well read too, and a good cook when his turn comes; he plays chess at just about my level of skill.

I already knew he wasn't from Earth, had in fact never been there, but from Aeneas, nearly 200 light-years distant, more than 300 from Lucifer. And, while he'd gotten an education at the new little university in Nova Roma, he was raised in the outback. Besides, that town is only a faroff colonial capital. It helped explain his utter commitment to belief in a God who became flesh and died for love of man. Not that I scoff. When he said his prayers, night and morning in our one-room shelter-dome, trustingly as a child, I didn't rag him nor he reproach me. Of course, over the weeks, we came more and more to talk about such matters.

At last he told me of that which haunted him.

We'd been out through the whole of one of Lucifer's long, long days; we'd toiled, we'd sweated, we'd itched and stunk and gotten grimy and staggered from weariness, we'd come near death once; and we'd found the uranium-concentrating root which was the key to the whole weirdness around us. We came back to base as day's fury was dying in the usual twilight gale; we washed, ate something, went to sleep with the hiss of storm-blown dust for a lullaby. Ten or twelve hours later we awoke and saw, through the vitryl panels, stars cold and crystalline beyond this thin air, auroras aflame, landscape hoar, and the twisted things we called trees all sheathed in glittering ice.

'Nothing we can do now till dawn,' I said, 'and we've earned a celebration.' So we prepared a large meal, elaborate as possible – breakfast or supper, what relevance had that here? We drank wine in the course of it, and afterward much brandy while we sat, side by side in our loungers, watching the march of constellations which Earth or Aeneas never saw. And we talked. Finally we talked of God.

' – maybe you can give me an idea,' Pete said. In the dim light, his face bore a struggle. He stared before him and knotted his fingers.

'M-m, I dunno,' I said carefully. 'To be honest, no offense meant, theological conundrums strike me as silly.'

He gave me a direct blue look. His tone was soft: 'That is, you feel the paradoxes don't arise if we don't insist on believing?'

'Yes. I respect your faith, Pete, but it's not mine. And if I did suppose a, well, a spiritual principle or something is behind the universe – ' I gestured at the high and terrible sky – 'in the name of reason, can we confine, can we understand whatever made *that*, in the bounds of one little dogma?'

'No. Agreed. How could finite minds grasp the infinite? We can see parts of it, though, that've been revealed to us.' He drew breath. ' 'Way back before space travel, the Church decided Jesus had come only to Earth, to man. If other intelligent races need salvation – and obviously a lot of them do! – God will have made His suitable arrangements for them. Sure. However, this does not mean Christianity is not true, or that certain different beliefs are not false.'

'Like, say, polytheism, wherever you find it?'

'I think so. Besides, religions evolve. The primitive faiths see God or the gods, as power; the higher ones see Him as justice; the highest see Him as love.' Abruptly he fell silent. I saw his fist clench, until he grabbed up his glass and drained it and refilled it in nearly a single savage motion.

'I must believe that,' he whispered.

I waited a few seconds, in Lucifer's crackling night stillness, before saying: 'An experience made you wonder?'

36

'Made me . . . disturbed. Mind if I tell you?'

'Certainly not.' I saw he was about to open himself; and I may be an unbeliever, but I know what is sacred.

'Happened about five years ago. I was on my first real job. So was the – ' his voice stumbled the least bit – 'the wife I had then. We were fresh out of school and apprenticeship, fresh into marriage.' In an effort at detachment: 'Our employers weren't human. They were Ythrians. Ever heard of them?'

I sought through my head. The worlds, races, beings are unknowably many, in this tiny corner of this one dust-mote galaxy which we have begun to explore a little. 'Ythrians . . . wait. Do they fly?'

'Yes. Surely one of the most glorious sights in creation. Your Ythrian isn't as heavy as a man, of course; adults mass around twenty-five or thirty kilos – but his wingspan goes up to six meters, and when he soars with those feathers shining gold-brown in the light, or stoops in a crack of thunder and whistle of wind— '

'Hold on,' I said. 'I take it Ythri's a terrestroid planet?'

'Pretty much. Somewhat smaller and drier than Earth, somewhat thinner atmosphere – about like Aeneas, in fact, which it's not too far from as interstellar spaces go. You can live there without special protection. The biochemistry's quite similar to ours.'

'Then how the devil can these creatures be that size? The wing loading's impossible, when you have only cell tissue to oxidize for power. They'd never get off the ground.'

'Ah, but they have antlibranchs as well.' Pete smiled, though it didn't go deep. 'Those look like three gills, sort of, on either side, below the wings. They're actually more like bellows, pumped by the wing muscles. Extra oxygen is forced directly into the bloodstream during flight. A biological supercharger system.'

'Well, I'll be a . . . never mind what.' I considered, in delight, this new facet of nature's inventivness. 'Um-m-m . . . if they spend energy at that rate, they've got to have appetites to match.'

'Right. They're carnivores. A number of them are still hunters. The advanced societies are based on ranching. In either case, obviously, it takes a lot of meat animals, a lot of square kilometers, to support one Ythrian. So they're fiercely territorial. They live in small groups – single families or extended households – which attack, with intent to kill, any uninvited outsider who doesn't obey an order to leave.'

'And still they're civilized enough to hire humans for space exploration?'

'Uh-huh. Remember, being flyers, they've never needed to huddle in cities in order to have ready communication. They do keep a few towns, mining or manufacturing centers, but those are inhabited mostly by wing-clipped slaves. I'm glad to say that institution's dying out as they get modern machinery.'

'By trade?' I guessed.

'Yes,' Pete replied. 'When the first Grand Survey discovered them, their most advanced culture was at an Iron Age level of technology; no industrial revolution, but plenty of sophisticated minds around, and subtle philosophies.' He paused. 'That's important to my question – that the Ythrians, at least of the Planha-speaking *choths,* are not barbarians and have not been for many centuries. They've had their equivalents of Socrates, Aristotle, Confucius, Galileo, yes, and their prophets and seers.'

After another mute moment: 'They realized early what the visitors from Earth implied, and set about attracting traders and teachers. Once they had some funds, they sent their promising young folk off-planet to study. I met several at my own university, which is why I got my job offer. By now they have a few spacecraft and native crews. But you'll understand, their technical people are spread thin, and in several branches of knowledge they have no experts. So they employ humans.'

He went on to describe the typical Ythrian: warm-blooded, feathered like a golden eagle (though more intricately) save for a crest on the head, and yet not a bird. Instead of a beak, a blunt muzzle full of fangs juts before two great eyes. The female bears her young alive. While she does not nurse them, they have lips to suck the juices of meat and fruits, wherefore their speech is not hopelessly unlike man's. What were formerly the legs have evolved into arms bearing three taloned fingers, flanked by two thumbs, on each hand. Aground, the huge wings

38

fold downward and, with the help of claws at the angles, give locomotion. That is slow and awkward – but aloft, ah!

'They become more alive, flying, than we ever do,' Pete murmured. His gaze had lost itself in the shuddering auroras overhead. 'They must: the metabolic rate they have then, and the space around them, speed, sky, a hundred winds to ride on and be kissed by . . . That's what made me think Enherrian, in particular, believed more keenly that I could hope to. I saw him and others dancing, high, high in the air, swoops, glides, hoverings, sunshine molten on their plumes; I asked what they did, and was told they were honoring God.'

He sighed. 'Or that's how I translated the Planha phrase, rightly or wrongly,' he went on. 'Olga and I had taken a cram course, and our Ythrian teammates all knew Anglic; but nobody's command of the foreign tongue was perfect. It couldn't be. Multiple billion years of separate existence, evolution, history – what a miracle that we could think as alike as we did!

'However, you could call Enherrian religious, same as you could call me that, and not be too grotesquely off the mark. The rest varied, just like humans. Some were also devout, some less, some agnostics or atheists; two were pagans, following the bloody rites of what was called the Old Faith. For that matter, my Olga – ' the knuckles stood forth where he grasped his tumbler of brandy – 'had tried, for my sake, to believe as I did, and couldn't.'

'Well. The New Faith interested me more. It was new only by comparison – at least as ancient as mine. I hoped for a chance to study it, to ask questions and compare ideas. I really knew nothing except that it was monotheistic, had sacraments and a theology though no official priesthood, upheld a high ethical and moral standard – for Ythrians, I mean. You can't expect a race which can only live by killing animals, and has an oestrous cycle, and is incapable by instinct of maintaining what we'd recognize as a true nation or government, and on and on – you can't expect them to resemble Christians much. God has given them a different message. I wished to know what. Surely we could learn from it.' Again he paused. 'After all . . . being a faith with a long tradition . . . and not static but a seeking, a history of prophets and saints and believers . . . I thought it

39

must know God is love. Now what form would God's love take to an Ythrian?'

He drank. I did too, before asking cautiously: 'Uh, where was this expedition?'

Pete stirred in his lounger. 'To a system about eighty light-years from Ythri's,' he answered. 'The original Survey crew had discovered a terrestroid planet there. They didn't bother to name it. Prospective colonists would choose their own name anyway. Those could be human or Ythrian, conceivably both – if the environment proved out.

'Offhand, the world – our group called it, unofficially, Gray, after that old captain – the world looked brilliantly promising. It's intermediate in size between Earth and Ythri, surface gravity 0.8 terrestrial; slightly more irradiation, from a some-what yellower sun, than Earth gets, which simply makes it a little warmer; axial tilt, therefore seasonal variations, a bit less than terrestrial; length of year about three-quarters of ours, length of day a bit under half; one small, close-in, bright moon; biochemistry similar to ours – we could eat most native things, though we'd require imported crops and livestock to supple-ment the diet. All in all, seemingly well-nigh perfect.'

'Rather remote to attract Earthlings at this early date,' I re-marked. 'And from your description, the Ythrians won't be able to settle it for quite a while either.'

'They think ahead,' Pete responded. 'Besides, they have scientific curiosity and, yes, in them perhaps even more than in humans who went along, a spirit of adventure. Oh, it was a wonderful thing to be young in that band!'

He had not yet reached thirty, but somehow his cry was not funny.

He shook himself. 'Well, we had to make sure,' he said. 'Besides planetology, ecology, chemistry, oceanography, meteor-ology, a million and a million mysteries to unravel for their own sakes – we must scout out the death traps, whatever those might be.

'At first everything went like Mary's smile on Christmas morning. The spaceship set us off – it couldn't be spared to linger in orbit – and we established base on the largest continent. Soon our hundred-odd dispersed across the globe, investigating

40

this or that. Olga and I made part of a group on the southern shore, where a great gulf swarmed with life. A strong current ran eastward from there, eventually striking an archipelago which deflected it north. Flying over those waters, we spied immense, I mean immense, patches – no, floating islands – of vegetation, densely interwoven, grazed on by monstrous marine creatures, no doubt supporting any number of lesser plant and animal speices.

'We wanted a close look. Our camp's sole aircraft wasn't good for that. Anyhow, it was already in demand for a dozen jobs. We had boats, though, and launched one. Our crew was Enherrian, his wife Whell, their grown children Rusa and Arrach, my beautiful new bride Olga, and me. We'd take three or four Gray days to reach the nearest atlantis weed, as Olga dubbed it. Then we'd be at least a week exploring before we turned back – a vacation, a lark, a joy.'

He tossed off his drink and reached for the bottle. 'You ran into grief,' I prompted.

'No.' He bent his lips upward, stiffly. 'It ran into us. A hurricane. Unpredicted; we knew very little about that planet. Given the higher solar energy input and, especially, the rapid rotation, the storm was more violent than would've been possible on Earth. We could only run before it and pray.

'At least, I prayed, and imagined that Enherrian did.'

Wind shrieked, hooted, yammered, hit flesh with fists and cold knives. Waves rumbled in that driven air, black and green and fang-white, fading from view as the sun sank behind the cloud-roil which hid it. Often a monster among them loomed castle-like over the gunwale. The boat slipped by, spilled into the troughs, rocked onto the crests and down again. Spindrift, icy, stinging, bitter on lips and tongue, made a fog across her length.

'We'll live if we can keep sea room,' Enherrian had said when the fury first broke. 'She's well-found. The engine capacitors have ample kilowatt-hours in them. Keep her bow on and we'll live.'

But the currents had them now, where the mighty gulfstream met the outermost islands and its waters churned, recoiled, spun about and fought. Minute by minute, the riptides grew wilder.

41

They made her yaw till she was broadside on and surges roared over her deck; they shocked her onto her beam ends, and the hull became a toning bell.

Pete, Olga, and Whell were in the cabin, trying to rest before their next watch. That was no longer possible. The Ythrian female locked hands and wing-claws around the net-covered framework wherein she had slept, hung on, and uttered nothing. In the wan glow of a single overhead fluoro, among thick restless shadows, her eyes gleamed topaz. They did not seem to look at the crampedness around – at what, then?

The humans had secured themselves by a line onto a lower bunk. They embraced, helping each other fight the leaps and swings which tried to smash them against the sides. Her fair hair on his shoulder was the last brightness in his cosmos. 'I love you,' she said, over and over, through hammerblows and groans. 'Whatever happens, I love you, Pete, I thank you for what you've given me.'

'And you,' he would answer. *And You*, he would think. *Though You won't take her, not yet, will You? Me, yes, if that's Your will. But not Olga. It'd leave Your creation too dark.*

A wing smote the cabin door. Barely to be heard through the storm, an Ythrian voice – high, whistly, but resonant out of full lungs – shouted: 'Come topside!'

Whell obeyed at once, the Bergs as fast as they could slip on life jackets. Having taken no personal grav units along, they couldn't fly free if they went overboard. Dusk raved around them. Pete could just see Rusa and Arrach in the stern, fighting the tiller. Enherrian stood before him and pointed forward. 'Look,' the captain said. Pete, who had no nictitating membranes, must shield eyes with fingers to peer athwart the hurricane. He saw a deeper darkness hump up from a wall of white; he heard surf crash.

'We can't pull free,' Enherrian told him. 'Between wind and current – too little power. We'll likely be wrecked. Make ready.'

Olga's hand went briefly to her mouth. She huddled against Pete and might have whispered, 'Oh, no.' Then she straightened, swung back down into the cabin, braced herself as best she could and started assembling the most vital things stored there. He saw that he loved her still more than he had known.

The same calm descended on him. Nobody had time to be afraid. He got busy too. The Ythrians could carry a limited weight of equipment and supplies, but sharply limited under these conditions. The humans, buoyed by their jackets, must carry most. They strapped it to their bodies.

When they re-emerged, the boat was in the shoals. Enherrian ordered them to take the rudder. His wife, son, and daughter stood around – on hands which clutched the rails with prey-snatching strength – and spread their wings to give a bit of shelter. The captain clung to the cabin top as lookout. His yelled commands reached the Bergs dim, tattered.

'Hard right!' Upwards cataracts burst on a skerry to port. It glided past, was lost in murk. 'Two points starboard – steady!' The hull slipped between a pair of rocks. Ahead was a narrow opening in the island's sheer black face. To a lagoon, to safety? Surf raged on either side of that gate, and everywhere else.

The passage was impossible. The boat struck, threw Olga off her feet and Arrach off her perch. Full reverse engine could not break loose. The deck canted. A billow and a billow smashed across.

Pete was in the water. It grabbed him, pulled him under, dragged him over a sharp bottom. He thought: *Into Your hands, God. Spare Olga, please, please* – and the sea spewed him back up for one gulp of air.

Wallowing in blindness, he tried to gauge how the breakers were acting, what he should do. If he could somehow belly-surf in, he might make it, he barely might . . . He was on the neck of a rushing giant, it climbed and climbed, it shoved him forward at what he knew was lunatic speed. He saw the reef on which it was about to smash him and knew he was dead.

Talons closed on his jacket. Air brawled beneath wings. The Ythrian could not raise him, but could draw him aside . . . the bare distance needed, and Pete went past the rock whereon his bones were to have been crushed, down into the smother and chaos beyond. The Ythrian didn't get free in time. He glimpsed the plumes go under, as he himself did. They never rose.

He beat on, and on, without end.

He floated in water merely choppy, swart palisades to right and left, a slope of beach ahead. He peered into the clamorous

43

dark and found nothing. 'Olga,' he croaked. 'Olga. Olga.'

Wings shadowed him among the shadows. 'Get ashore before an undertow eats you!' Enherrian whooped, and beat his way off in search.

Pete crawled to gritty sand, fell, and let annihilation have him. He wasn't unconscious long. When he revived, Rusa and Whell were beside him. Enherrian was further inland. The captain hauled on a line he had snubbed around a tree. Olga floated at the other end. She had no strength left, but he had passed a bight beneath her arms and she was alive.

At wolf-gray dawn the wind had fallen to gale force or maybe less, and the cliffs shielded lagoon and strand from it. Overhead it shrilled, and outside the breakers cannonaded, their rage aquiver through the island. Pete and Olga huddled together, a shared cloak across their shoulders. Enherrian busied himself checking the salvaged material. Whell sat on the hindbones of her wings and stared seaward. Moisture gleamed on her grizzled feathers like tears.

Rusa flew in from the reefs and landed. 'No trace,' he said. His voice was emptied by exhaustion. 'Neither the boat nor Arrach.' Through the rust in his own brain, Pete noticed the order of those words.

Nevertheless -- He leaned toward the parents and brother of Arrach, who had been beautiful and merry and had sung to them by moonlight. 'How can we say – ?' he began, realized he didn't have Planha words, and tried in Anglic: 'How can we say how sorry we both are?'

'No necessity,' Rusa answered.

'She died saving me!'

'And what you were carrying, which we needed badly.' Some energy returned to Rusa. He lifted his head and its crest. 'She had deathpride, our lass.'

Afterward Pete, in his search for meaning, would learn about that Ythrian concept. 'Courage' is too simple and weak a translation. Certain Old Japanese words come closer, though they don't really bear the same value either.

Whell turned her hawk gaze full upon him. 'Did you see anything of what happened in the water?' she asked. He was too

44

unfamiliar with her folk to interpret the tone: today he thinks it was loving. He did know that, being creatures of seasonal rut, Ythrians are less sexually motivated than man is, but probably treasure their young even more. The strongest bond between male and female is children, who are what life is all about.

'No, I . . . I fear not,' he stammered.

Enherrian reached out to lay claws, very gently and briefly, on his wife's back. 'Be sure she fought well,' he said. 'She gave God honor.' (Glory? Praise? Adoration? His due?)

Does he mean she prayed, made her confession, while she drowned? The question dragged itself through Pete's weariness and caused him to murmur: 'She's in heaven now.' Again he was forced to use Anglic words.

Enherrian gave him a look which he could have sworn was startled: 'What do you say? Arrach is dead.'

'Why, her . . . her spirit –'

'Will be remembered in pride.' Enherrian resumed his work.

Olga said it for Pete: 'So you don't believe the spirit outlives the body?'

'How could it?' Enherrian snapped. 'Why should it?' His motions, his posture, the set of his plumage added: Leave me alone.

Pete thought: *Well, many faiths, including high ones, including some sects which call themselves Christian, deny immortality. How sorry I feel for these my friends, who don't know they will meet their beloved afresh!*

They will, regardless. It makes no sense that God, Who created what is because in His goodness he wished to share existence, would shape a soul only to break it and throw it away.

Never mind. The job on hand is to keep Olga alive, in her dear body. 'Can I help?'

'Yes, check our medical kit,' Enherrian said.

It had come through undamaged in its box. The items for human use – stimulants, sedatives, anesthetics, antitoxins, antibiotics, coagulants, healing promoters, et standard cetera – naturally outnumbered those for Ythrians. There hasn't been time to develop a large scientific pharmacopoeia for the latter species. True, certain materials work on both, as does the surgical and monitoring equipment. Pete distributed pills which took the pain out of bruises and scrapes, the heaviness out of muscles. Meanwhile Rusa collected wood, Whell started and tended a fire, Olga made breakfast. They had considerable food, mostly freeze-dried, gear to cook it, tools like knives and a hatchet, cord, cloth, flashbeams, two blasters and abundant recharges: what they required for survival.

'It may be insufficient,' Enherrian said. 'The portable radio transceiver went down with Arrach. The boats' transmitter couldn't punch a call through that storm, and now the boat's on the bottom – nothing to see from the air, scant metal to register on a detector.'

'Oh, they'll check on us when the weather slacks off,' Olga said. She caught Pete's hand in hers. He felt the warmth.

'If their flitter survived the hurricane, which I doubt,' Enherrian stated. 'I'm convinced the camp was also struck. We had built no shelter for the flitter, our people will have been too busy saving themselves to secure it, and I think that thin shell was tumbled about and broken. If I'm right, they'll have to call for an aircraft from elsewhere, which may not be available at once. In either case, we could be anywhere in a huge territory; and the expedition has no time or personnel for an indefinite search. They will seek us, aye; however, if we are not found before an abitrary date – ' A ripple passed over the feathers of face and neck; a human would have shrugged.

'What . . . can we do?' the girl asked.

'Clear a sizeable area in a plainly artificial pattern, or heap fuel for beacon fires should a flitter pass within sight – whichever is practicable. If nothing comes of that, we should consider building a raft or the like.'

'Or modify a life jacket for me,' Rusa suggested, 'and I can try to fly to the mainland.'

Enherrian nodded. 'We must investigate the possibilities. First let's get a real rest.'

The Ythrians were quickly asleep, squatted on their locked wing joints like idols of a forgotten people. Pete and Olga felt more excited and wandered a distance off, hand in hand.

Above the crag-enclosed beach, the island rose toward a crest which he estimated as three kilometers away. If it was in the middle, this was no large piece of real estate. Nor did he see adequate shelter. A mat of mossy, intensely green plants squeezed out any possibility of forest. A few trees stood isolated. Their branches tossed in the wind. He noticed particularly one atop a great outcrop nearby, gaunt brown trunk and thin leaf-fringed boughs that whipped insanely about. Blossoms, torn from vines, blew past, and they were gorgeous; but there would be naught to live on here, and he wasn't hopeful about learning, in time, how to catch Gray's equivalent of fish.

'Strange about them, isn't it?' Olga murmured.

'Eh?' He came, startled, out of his preoccupations.

She gestured at the Ythrians. 'Them. The way they took poor Arrach's death.'

'Well, you can't judge them by our standards. Maybe they feel grief less than we would, or maybe their culture demands stoicism.' He looked at her and did not look away again. 'To be frank, darling, I can't really mourn either. I'm too happy to have you back.'

'And I you – oh, Pete, Pete, my only – '

They found a secret spot and made love. He saw nothing wrong in that. Do you ever in this life come closer to the wonder which is God?

Afterward they returned to their companions. Thus the clash of wings awoke them, hours later. They scrambled from their bedrolls and saw the Ythrians swing aloft.

The wind was strong and loud as yet, though easing off in fickleness, flaws, downdrafts, whirls, and eddies. Clouds were mostly gone. Those which remained raced gold and hot orange before a sun low in the west, across blue serenity. The lagoon glittered purple, the greensward lay aglow. It had warmed up till rich odors of growth, of flowers, blent with the sea-salt.

And splendid in the sky danced Enherrian, Whell, and Rusa. They wheeled, soared, pounced, and rushed back into light which ran molten off their pinions. They chanted, and fragments blew down to the humans: *'High flew your spirit on many winds . . . be always remembered . . .'*

'What *is* that?' Olga breathed.

'Why, they – they – ' The knowledge broke upon Pete. 'They're holding a service for Arrach.'

He knelt and said a prayer for her soul's repose. But he wondered if she, who had belonged to the air, would truly want rest. And his eyes could not leave her kindred.

Enherrian screamed a hunter's challenge and rushed down at the earth. He flung himself meteoric past the stone outcrop Pete had seen; for an instant the man gasped, believing he would be shattered; then he rose, triumphant.

He passed by the lean tree of thin branches. Gusts flailed them about. A nearly razor edge took off his left wing. Blood spurted; Ythrian blood is royal purple. Somehow Enherrian slewed around and made a crash landing on the bluff top, just beyond range of what has since been named the surgeon tree.

Pete yanked the medikit to him and ran. Olga wailed, briefly, and followed. When they reached the scene, they found that Whell and Rusa had pulled feathers from their breasts to try staunching the wound.

Evening, night, day, evening, night.

Enherrian sat before a campfire. Its light wavered, picked him red out of shadow and let him half-vanish again, save for the unblinking yellow eyes. His wife and son supported him. Stim, cell-freeze, and plasma surrogate had done their work, and he could speak in a weak roughness. The bandages on his stump were a nearly glaring white.

Around crowded shrubs which, by day, showed low and russet-leaved. They filled a hollow on the far side of the island, to which Enherrian had been carried on an improvised litter. Their odor was rank, in an atmosphere once more subtropically hot, and they clutched at feet with raking twigs. But this was the most sheltered spot his companions could find, and he might die in a new storm on the open beach.

He looked through smoke, at the Bergs, who sat as close together as they were able. He said – the surf growled faintly beneath his words, while never a leaf rustled in the breathless dark – 'I have read that your people can make a lost part grow forth afresh.'

Pete couldn't answer. He tried but couldn't. It was Olga who had the courage to say, 'We can do it for ourselves. None

48

except ourselves.' She laid her head on her man's breast and wept.

Well, you need a lot of research to unravel a genetic code, a lot of development to make the molecules of heredity repeat what they did in the womb. Science hasn't had time yet for other races. It never will for all. They are too many.

'As I thought,' Enherrian said. 'Nor can a proper prosthesis be engineered in my lifetime. I have few years left; an Ythrian who cannot fly soon becomes sickly.'

'Grav units – ' Pete faltered.

The scorn in those eyes was like a blow. Dead metal to raise you, who have had wings?

Fierce and haughty though the Ythrian is, his quill-clipped slaves have never rebelled: for they are only half-alive. Imagine yourself, human male, castrated. Enherrian might flap his remaining wing and the stump to fill his blood with air; but he would have nothing he could do with that extra energy, it would turn inward and corrode his body, perhaps at last his mind.

For a second, Whell laid an arm around him.

'You will devise a signal tomorrow,' Enherrian said, 'and start work on it. Too much time has already been wasted.'

Before they slept, Pete managed to draw Whell aside. 'He needs constant care, you know,' he whispered to her in the acrid booming gloom. 'The drugs got him over the shock, but he can't tolerate more and he'll be very weak.'

True, she said with feathers rather than voice. Aloud: 'Olga shall nurse him. She cannot get around as easily as Rusa or me, and lacks your physical strength. Besides, she can prepare meals and the like for us.'

Pete nodded absently. He had a dread to explain. 'Uh . . . uh . . . do you think – well, I mean in your ethic, in the New Faith – might Enherrian put an end to himself?' And he wondered if God would really blame the captain.

Her wings and tail spread, her crest erected, she glared. 'You say that of him?' she shrilled. Seeing his concern, she eased, even made a *krrr* noise which might answer to a chuckle. 'No, no, he has his deathpride. He would never rob God of honor.'

After survey and experiment, the decision was to hack a giant cross in the island turf. That growth couldn't be ignited, and what wood was burnable – deadfall – was too scant and stingy of smoke for a beacon.

The party had no spades; the vegetable mat was thick and tough; the toil became brutal. Pete, like Whell and Rusa, would return to camp and topple into sleep. He wouldn't rouse till morning, to gulp his food and plod off to labor. He grew gaunt, bearded, filthy, numb-brained, sore in every cell.

Thus he did not notice how Olga was waning. Enherrian was mending, somewhat, under her care. She did her jobs, which were comparatively light, and would have been ashamed to complain of headaches, giddiness, diarrhea, and nausea. Doubtless she imagined she suffered merely from reaction to disaster, plus a sketchy and ill-balanced diet, plus heat and brilliant sun and – She'd cope.

The days were too short for work, the nights too short for sleep. Pete's terror was that he would see a flitter pass and vanish over the horizon before the Ythrians could hail it. Then they might try sending Rusa for help. But that was a long, tricky flight; and the gulf coast camp was due to be struck rather soon anyway.

Sometimes he wondered dimly how he and Olga might do if marooned on Gray. He kept enough wits to dismiss his fantasy for what it was. Take the simple fact that native life appeared to lack certain vitamins –

Then one darkness, perhaps a terrestrial week after the shipwreck, he was roused by her crying his name. He struggled to wakefulness. She lay beside him. Gray's moon was up, nearly full, swifter and brighter than Luna. Its glow drowned most of the stars, frosted the encroaching bushes, fell without pity to show him her fallen cheeks and rolling eyes. She shuddered in his arms; he heard her teeth clapping. 'I'm cold, darling, I'm cold,' she said in the subtropical summer night. She vomited over him, and presently she was delirious.

The Ythrians gave what help they could, he what medicines he could. By sunrise (an outrageousness of rose and gold and silver-blue, crossed by the jubilant wings of waterfowl) he knew she was dying.

He examined his own physical state, using a robot he discovered he had in his skull: yes, his wretchedness was due to more than overwork, he saw that now; he too had had the upset stomach and the occasional shivers, nothing like the disintegration which possessed Olga, nevertheless the same kind of thing. Yet the Ythrians stayed healthy. Did a local germ attack humans while finding the other race undevourable?

The rescuers, who came on the island two Gray days later, already had the answer. That genus of bushes is widespread on the planet. A party elsewhere, after getting sick and getting into safety suits, analyzed its vapors. They are a cumulative poison to man; they scarcely harm an Ythrian. The analysts named it the hell shrub.

Unfortunately, their report wasn't broadcast until after the boat left. Meanwhile Pete had been out in the field every day, while Olga spent her whole time in the hollow, over which the sun regularly created an inversion layer.

Whell and Rusa went grimly back to work. Pete had to get away. He wasn't sure of the reason, but he had to be alone when he screamed at heaven, 'Why did You do this to her, why did You do it?' Enherrian could look after Olga, who had brought him back to a life he no longer wanted. Pete had stopped her babblings, writhings, and sawtoothed sounds of pain with a shot. She ought to sleep peacefully into that death which the monitor instruments said was, in the absence of hospital facilities, ineluctable.

He stumbled off to the heights. The sea reached calm, in a thousand hues of azure and green, around the living island, beneath the gentle sky. He knelt in all that emptiness and put his question.

After an hour he could say, 'Your will be done' and return to camp.

Olga lay awake. 'Pete, Pete!' she cried. Anguish distorted her voice till he couldn't recognize it; nor could he really see her in the yellowed sweating skin and lank hair drawn over a skeleton, or find her in the stench and the nails which flayed him as they clutched. 'Where were you, hold me close, it hurts, how it hurts –'

He gave her a second injection, to small effect.

51

He knelt again, beside her. He has not told me what he said, or how. At last she grew quiet, gripped him hard and waited for the pain to end.

When she died, he says, it was like seeing a light blown out.

He laid her down, closed eyes and jaw, folded her hands. On mechanical feet he went to the pup tent which had been rigged for Enherrian. The cripple calmly awaited him. 'She is fallen?' he asked.

Pete nodded.

'That is well,' Enherrian said.

'It is not,' Pete heard himself reply, harsh and remote. 'She shouldn't have aroused. The drug should've – Did you give her a stim shot? Did you bring her back to suffer?'

'What else?' said Enherrian, though he was unarmed and a blaster lay nearby for Pete to seize. *Not that I'll ease* him *out of his fate!* went through the man in a spasm. 'I saw that you, distraught, had misgauged. You were gone and I unable to follow you. She might well die before your return.'

Out of his void, Pete gaped into those eyes. 'You mean,' rattled from him, 'you mean . . . she . . . mustn't?'

Enherrian crawled forth – he could only crawl, on his single wing – to take Pete's hands. 'My friend,' he said, his tone immeasurably compassionate, 'I honored you both too much to deny her her deathpride.'

Pete's chief awareness was of the cool sharp talons.

'Have I misunderstood?' asked Enherrian anxiously. 'Did you not wish her to give God a battle?'

Even on Lucifer, the nights finally end. Dawn blazed on the tors when Pete finished his story.

I emptied the last few cc. into our glasses. We'd get no work done today. 'Yeh,' I said. 'Cross-cultural semantics. Given the best will in the universe, two beings from different planets – or just different countries, often – take for granted they think alike; and the outcome can be tragic.'

'I assumed that at first,' Pete said. 'I didn't need to forgive Enherrian – how could he know? For his part, he was puzzled when I buried my darling. On Ythri they cast them from a great height into wilderness. But neither race wants to watch the

52

rotting of what was loved, so he did his lame best to help me.'

He drank, looked as near the cruel bluish sun as he was able, and mumbled: 'What I couldn't do was forgive God.'

'The problem of evil,' I said.

'Oh, no. I've studied these matters, these past years: read theology, argued with priests, the whole route. Why does God, if He is a loving and personal God, allow evil? Well, there's a perfectly good Christian answer to that. Man — intelligence everywhere — must have free will. Otherwise we're puppets and have no reason to exist. Free will necessarily includes the capability of doing wrong. We're here, in this cosmos during our lives, to learn how to be good of our unforced choice.'

'I spoke illiterately,' I apologized. 'All that brandy. No, sure, your logic is right, regardless of whether I accept your premises or not. What I meant was: the problem of pain. Why does a merciful God permit undeserved agony? If He's omnipotent, He isn't compelled to.

'I'm not talking about the sensation which warns you to take your hand from the fire, anything useful like that. No, the random accident which wipes out a life . . . or a mind — ' I drank. 'What happened to Arrach, yes, and to Enherrian, and Olga, and you, and Whell. What happens when a disease hits, or those catastrophes we label acts of God. Or the slow decay of us if we grow very old. Every such horror. Never mind if science has licked some of them; we have enough left, and then there were our ancestors who endured them all.

'Why? What possible end is served? It's not adequate to declare we'll receive an unbounded reward after we die and therefore it makes no difference whether a life was gusty or grisly. That's no explanation.

'Is this the problem you're grappling with, Pete?'

'In a way.' He nodded, cautiously, as if he were already his father's age. 'At least, it's the start of the problem.

'You see, there I was, isolated among Ythrians. My fellow humans sympathized, but they had nothing to say that I didn't know already. The New Faith, however . . . Mind you, I wasn't about to convert. What I did hope for was an insight, a freshness, that'd help me make Christian sense of our losses. Enherrian was so sure, so learned, in his beliefs –

'We talked, and talked, and talked, while I was regaining my strength. He was as caught as me. Not that he couldn't fit our troubles into his scheme of things. That was easy. But it turned out that the New Faith has no satisfactory answer to the problem of *evil*. It says God allows wickedness so we may win honor by fighting for the right. Really, when you stop to think, that's weak, especially in carnivore Ythrian terms. Don't you agree?'

'You know them, I don't,' I sighed. 'You imply they have a better answer to the riddle of pain than your own religion does.'

'It seems better.' Desperation edged his slightly blurred tone:

'They're hunters, or were until lately. They see God like that, as the Hunter. Not the Torturer – you absolutely must understand this point – no, He rejoices in our happiness the way we might rejoice to see a game animal gamboling. Yet at last He comes after us. Our noblest moment is when we, knowing He is irresistible, give Him a good chase, a good fight.

'Then He wins honor. And some infinite end is furthered. (The same one as when my God is given praise? How can I tell?) We're dead, struck down, lingering at most a few years in the memories of those who escaped this time. And that's what we're here for. That's why God created the universe.'

'And this belief is old,' I said. 'It doesn't belong just to a few cranks. No, it's been held for centuries by millions of sensitive, intelligent, educated beings. You can live by it, you can die by it. If it doesn't solve every paradox, it solves some that your faith won't, quite. This is your dilemma, true?'

He nodded again. 'The priests have told me to deny a false creed and to acknowledge a mystery. Neither instruction feels right. Or am I asking too much?'

'I'm sorry, Pete,' I said, altogether honestly. It hurt. 'But how should I know? I looked into the abyss once, and saw nothing, and haven't looked since. You keep looking. Which of us is the braver?

'Maybe you can find a text in Job. I don't know, I tell you, I don't know.'

The sun lifted higher above the burning horizon.

What Rennhi, her flightmates in the endeavor, and more lately Hloch were able to seek out has been limited and in great measure chance-blown. No scholar from Avalon has yet prevailed over the time or the means to ransack data banks on Terra itself. Yonder must abide records more full by a cloud-height than those which have reached the suns where Domain of Ythri and Terran Empire come together.

It may be just as well. They would surely overwhelm the writer of this book, whose aim is at no more than an account of certain human events which helped bring about the founding of the Stormgate Choth. Even the fragmentary original material he has is more than he can directly use. He rides among whatever winds blow, choosing first one, then another, hoping that in this wise he may find the overall set of the airstream.

Here is a story of no large import, save that it gives a picture from within of Terran society when the Polesotechnic League was in its glory – and, incidentally, makes the first mention known to Hloch of a being who was to take a significant part in later history. The source is a running set of reminiscences written down through much of his life by James Ching, a spaceman who eventually settled on Catawrayannis. His descendants kept the notebooks and courteously made them available to Rennhi after she had heard of their existence. To screen a glossary of obscure terms, punch Library Central 254-0691.

HOW TO BE ETHNIC IN ONE
EASY LESSON

Adzel talks a lot about blessings in disguise, but this disguise
was impenetrable. In fact, what Simon Snyder handed me was
an exploding bomb.

I was hard at study when my phone warbled. That alone
jerked me half out of my lounger. I'd set that instrument to pass
calls from no more than a dozen people, to all of whom I'd
explained that they shouldn't bother me about anything much
less urgent than a rogue planet on a collision course.

You see, my preliminary tests for the Academy were coming
up soon. Not the actual entrance exams – I'd face those a year
hence – but the tests as to whether I should be allowed to apply
for admission. You can't blame that policy on the Brotherhood. Not many regular spacemen's berths become available
annually, and a hundred young Earthlings clamor for each of
them. The ninety-nine who don't make it . . . well, mostly they
try to get work with some company which will maybe someday
assign them to a post somewhere outsystem; or they set their
teeth and save their money till at last they can go as shepherded
tourists.

At night, out above the ocean in my car, away from city
glow, I'd look upward and be ripped apart by longing. As for
the occasional trips to Luna – last time, several months before,
I'd found my eyes running over at sight of that sky, when the
flit was my sixteenth-birthday present.

And now tensor calculus was giving me trouble. No doubt the
Education Central computer would have gotten monumentally
bored, projecting the same stuff over and over on my screen, if

it had been built to feel emotions. Is that why it hasn't been?

The phone announced: 'Freeman Snyder.'

You don't refuse your principal counselor. His or her word has too much to do with the evaluation of you as a potential student by places like the Academy. 'Accept,' I gulped. As his lean features flashed on: 'Greeting, sir.'

'Greeting, Jim,' he said. 'How are you?'

'Busy,' I hinted.

'Indeed. You are a rather intense type, eh? The indices show you're apt to work yourself into the ground. A change of pace is downright necessary.'

Why are we saddled with specialists who arbite our lives on the basis of a psychoprofile and a theory? If I'd been apprenticed to a Master Merchant of the Polesotechnic League instead, he wouldn't have given two snorts in vacuum about my 'optimum developmental strategy'. He'd have told me, 'Ching, do this or learn that'; and if I didn't cut it satisfactorily, I'd be fired – or dead, because we'd be on strange worlds, out among the stars, the stars.

No use daydreaming. League apprenticeships are scarcer than hair on a neutron, and mostly filled by relatives. (That's less nepotism for its own sake than a belief that kin of survivor types are more likely to be the same than chance-met groundhugger kids.) I was an ordinary student bucking for an Academy appointment, from which I'd graduate to service on regular runs and maybe, at last, a captaincy.

'To be frank,' Simon Snyder went on, 'I've worried about your indifference to extracurricular activities. It doesn't make for an outgoing personality, you know. I've thought of an undertaking which should be right in your orbit. In addition, it'll be a real service, it'll bring real credit, to – ' he smiled afresh to pretend he was joking while he intoned – 'the educational complex of San Francisco Integrate.'

'I haven't time!' I wailed.

'Certainly you do. You can't study twenty-four hours a day, even if a medic would prescribe the stim. Brains go stale. All work and no play, remember. Besides, Jim, this matter has its serious aspect. I'd like to feel I could endorse your altruism as well as your technological abilities.'

I eased my muscles, let the lounger mold itself around me, and said in what was supposed to be a hurrah voice: 'Please tell me, Freeman Snyder.'

He beamed. 'I knew I could count on you. You've heard of the upcoming Festival of Man.'

'Haven't I?' Realizing how sour my tone was, I tried again. 'I have.'

He gave me a pretty narrow look. 'You don't sound too enthusiastic.'

'Oh, I'll tune in ceremonies and such, catch a bit of music and drama and whatnot, if and when the chance comes. But I've got to get these transformations in hyperdrive theory straight, or – '

'I'm afraid you don't quite appreciate the importance of the Festival, Jim. It's more than a set of shows. It's an affirmation.'

Yes, I'd heard that often enough before – too dismally often. Doubtless you remember the line of argument the promoters used: 'Humankind, gaining the stars, is in grave danger of losing its soul. Our extraterrestrial colonies are fragmenting into new nations, whole new cultures, to which Earth is scarcely a memory. Our traders, our explorers push ever outward, ever further away; and no missionary spirit drives them, nothing but lust for profit and adventure. Meanwhile the Solar Commonwealth is deluged with alien – nonhuman – influence, not only diplomats, entrepreneurs, students, and visitors, but the false glamour of ideas never born on man's true home – We grant we have learned much of value from these outsiders. But much else has been unassimilable or has had a disastrously distorting effect, especially in the arts. Besides, they are learning far more from us. Let us proudly affirm that fact. Let us hark back to our own origins, our variousness. Let us strike new roots in the soil from which our forebears sprang.'

A year-long display of Earth's past – well, it'd be colorful, if rather fakey most of the time. I couldn't take it more seriously than that. Space was where the future lay, I thought. At least, it was where I dreamed my personal future would lie. What were dead bones to me, no matter how fancy the costumes you put on them? Not that I scorned the past; even then, I wasn't so foolish. I just believed that what was worth saving would save itself, and the rest had better be let fade away quietly.

I tried to explain to my counselor: 'Sure, I've been told about "culture pseudomorphosis" and the rest. Really, though, Freeman Snyder, don't you think the shoe is on the other foot? Like, well, I've got this friend from Woden, name of Adzel, here to learn planetology. That's a science we developed; his folk are primitive hunters, newly discovered by us. He talks human languages too – he's quick at languages – and lately he was converted to Buddhism and – Shouldn't the Wodenites worry about being turned into imitation Earthlings?'

My example wasn't the best, because you can only humanize a four-and-a-half-meter-long dragon to a limited extent. Whether he knew that or not (who can know all the races, all the worlds we've already found in our small corner of this wonderful cosmos?) Snyder wasn't impressed. He snapped, 'The sheer variety of extraterrestrial influence is demoralizing. Now I want our complex to make a decent showing during the Festival. Every department, office, club, church, institution in the Integrate will take part. I want its schools to have a leading role.'

'Don't they, sir? I mean, aren't projects under way?'

'Yes, yes, to a degree.' He waved an impatient hand. 'Far less than I'd expect from our youth. Too many of you are spacestruck— ' He checked himself, donned his smile again, and leaned forward till his image seemed ready to fall out of the screen. 'I've been thinking about what my own students might do. In your case, I have a first-class idea. You will represent San Francisco's Chinese community among us.'

'What?' I yelped. 'But – but – '

'A very old, almost unique tradition,' he said. 'Your people have been in this area for five or six hundred years.'

'*My* people?' The room wobbled around me. 'I mean . . . well, sure, my name's Ching and I'm proud of it. And maybe the, uh, the chromosome recombinations do make me look like those ancestors. But . . . half a thousand years, sir! If I haven't got blood in me of every breed of human being that ever lived, why, then I'm a statistical monstrosity!'

'True. However, the accident which makes you a throwback to your Mongoloid forebears is helpful. Few of my students are identifiably anything. I try to find roles for them, on the basis of surnames, but it isn't easy.'

Yeh, I thought bitterly. *By your reasoning everybody named Marcantonio should dress in a toga for the occasion, and everybody named Smith should paint himself blue.*

'There is a local ad hoc committee on Chinese-American activities,' Snyder went on. 'I suggest you contact them and ask for ideas and information. What can you present on behalf of our educational system? And then, of course, there's Library Central. It can supply more historical material than you could read in a lifetime. Do you good to learn a few subjects besides math, physics, xenology – ' His grimace passed by. I gave him marks for sincerity: 'Perhaps you can devise something, a float or the like, something which will call on your engineering ingenuity and knowledge. That would please them too, when you apply at the Academy.'

Sure, I thought, *if it hasn't eaten so much of my time that I flunk these prelims.*

'Remember,' Snyder said, 'the Festival opens in barely three months. I'll expect progress reports from you. Feel free to call on me for help or advice at any time. That's what I'm here for, you know: to guide you in developing your whole self.'

More of the same followed. I haven't the stomach to record it.

I called Betty Riefenstahl, but just to find out if I could come see her. Though holovids are fine for image and sound, you can't hold hands with one or catch a whiff of perfume and girl.

Her phone told me she wasn't available till evening. That gave me ample chance to gnaw my nerves raw. I couldn't flat-out refuse Snyder's pet notion. The right was mine, of course, and he wouldn't consciously hold a grudge; but neither would he speak as well as he might of my energy and team spirit. On the other hand, what did I know about Chinese civilization? I'd seen the standard sights; I'd read a classic or two in literature courses; and that was that. What persons I'd met over there were as modern-oriented as myself. (No pun, I hope!) And as for Chinese-Americans –

Vaguely remembering that San Francisco had once had

special ethnic sections, I did ask Library Central. It screened a fleet of stuff about a district known as Chinatown. Probably contemporaries found that area picturesque. (Oh, treetop highways under the golden-red sun of Cynthia! Four-armed drummers who sound the mating call of Gorzun's twin moons! Wild wings above Ythri!) The inhabitants had celebrated a Lunar New Year with fireworks and a parade. I couldn't make out details – the photographs had been time-blurred when their information was recoded – and was too disheartened to plow through the accompanying text.

For me, dinner was a refueling stop. I mumbled something to my parents, who mean well but can't understand why I must leave the nice safe Commonwealth, and flitted off to the Riefenstahl place.

The trip calmed me a little. I was reminded that, to outworlders like Adzel, the miracle was here. Light glimmered in a million earthbound stars across the hills, far out over the great sheen of Bay and ocean; often it fountained upward in a many-armed tower, often gave way to the sweet darkness of a park or ecocenter. A murmur of machines beat endlessly through cool, slightly foggy air. Traffic Control passed me so near a bus that I looked in its canopy and saw the passengers were from the whole globe and beyond – a dandified Lunarian, a stocky blue-skin of Alfzar, a spacehand identified by his Brotherhood badge, a journeyman merchant of the Polesotechnic League who didn't bother with any identification except the skin weathered beneath strange suns, the go-to-hell independence in his face, which turned me sick with envy.

The Riefenstahl's apartment overlooked the Golden Gate. I saw lights twinkle and flare, heard distant clangor and hissing, where crews worked around the clock to replicate an ancient bridge. Betty met me at the door. She's slim and blonde and usually cheerful. Tonight she looked so tired and troubled that I myself paid scant attention to the briefness of her tunic.

'Sh!' she cautioned. 'Let's don't say hello to Dad right now. He's in his study, and it's very brown.' I knew that her mother was away from home, helping develop the tape of a modern musical composition. Her father conducted the San Francisco Opera.

She led me to the living room, sat me down, and punched for coffee. A full-wall transparency framed her where she continued standing, in city glitter and shimmer, a sickle moon with a couple of pinpoint cities visible on its dark side, a few of the brightest stars. 'I'm glad you came, Jimmy,' she said. 'I need a shoulder to cry on.'

'Like me,' I answered. 'You first, however.'

'Well, it's Dad. He's ghastly worried. This stupid Festival – '

'Huh?' I searched my mind and found nothing except the obvious. 'Won't he be putting on a, uh, Terrestrial piece?'

'He's expected to. He's been researching till every hour of the mornings, poor dear. I've been helping him go through playbacks – hundreds and hundreds of years' worth – and prepare synopses and excerpts to show the directors. We only finished yesterday, and I *had* to catch up on sleep. That's why I couldn't let you come earlier.'

'But what's the problem?' I asked. 'Okay, you've been forced to scan those tapes. But once you've picked your show, you just project it, don't you? At most, you may need to update the language. And you've got your mother to handle reprogramming.'

Betty sighed. 'It's not that simple. You see, they – his board of directors, plus the officials in charge of San Francisco's participation – they insist on a live performance.'

Partly I knew what she was talking about, partly she explained further. Freeman Riefenstahl had pioneered the revival of in-the-flesh opera. Yes, he said, we have holographic records of the greatest artists; yes, we can use computers to generate original works and productions which no mortal being could possibly match. Yet neither approach will bring forth new artists with new concepts of a part, nor do they give individual brains a chance to create – and, when a million fresh ideas are flowing in to us from the galaxy, natural-born genius must create or else revolt.

'Let us by all means use technical tricks where they are indicated, as for special effects,' Freeman Riefenstahl said. 'But let us never forget that music is only alive in a living performer.' While I don't claim to be very esthetic, I tuned in his shows whenever I could. They did have an excitement which no tape and no calculated stimulus interplay – no matter how excellent – can duplicate.

'His case is like yours,' Betty told me near the start of our acquaintance. 'We could send robots to space. Nevertheless men go, at whatever risk.' That was when I stopped thinking of her as merely pretty.

Tonight, her voice gone bleak, she said: 'Dad succeeded too well. He's been doing contemporary things, you know, letting the archives handle the archaic. Now they insist he won't be showing sufficient respect, as a representative of the Integrate, for the Human Ethos – unless he puts on a historic item, live, as the Opera Company's share of the Festival.'

'Well, can't he?' I asked. 'Sure, it's kind of short notice, same as for me. Still, given modern training methods for his cast – '

'Of course, of course,' she said irritably. 'But don't you see, a routine performance isn't good enough either? People today are conditioned to visual spectacles. At least, the directors claim so. And – Jimmy, the Festival is important, if only because of the publicity. If Dad's part in it falls flat, his contract may not be renewed. Certainly his effort would be hurt, to educate the public back to real music.' Her tone and her head drooped. 'And that'd hurt him.'

She drew a breath, straightened, even coaxed a smile into existence. 'Well, we've made our précis of suggestions,' she said. 'We're waiting to hear what the board decides, which may take days. Meanwhile, you need to tell me your woes.' Sitting down opposite me: 'Do.'

I obeyed. At the end I grinned on one side of my face and remarked: 'Ironic, huh? Here your father has to stage an ultra-ethnic production – I'll bet they'll turn handsprings for him if he can make it German, given a name like his – only he's not supposed to use technology for much except backdrops. And here I have to do likewise, in Chinese style, the flashier the better, only I really haven't time to apply the technology for making a firework fountain or whatever. Maybe he and I should pool our efforts.'

'How?'

'I dunno.' I shifted in the chair. 'Let's get out of here, go someplace where we can forget this mess.'

What I had in mind was a flit over the ocean or down to the swimmably warm waters off Baja, followed maybe by a snack in a restaurant featuring outsystem food. Betty gave me no chance. She nodded and said quickly, 'Yes, I've been wanting to. A serene environment – Do you think Adzel might be at home?'

The League scholarship he'd wangled back on his planet didn't reach far on Earth, especially when he had about a ton of warm-blooded mass to keep fed. He couldn't afford special quarters, or anything near the Clement Institute of Planetology. Instead, he paid exorbitant rent for a shack 'way down in the San Jose district. The sole public transportation he could fit into was a rickety old twice-a-day gyrotrain, which meant he lost hours commuting to his laboratory and live-lecture classes, waiting for them to begin and waiting around after they were finished. Also, I strongly suspected he was undernourished. I'd fretted about him ever since we met, in the course of a course in micrometrics.

He always dismissed my fears: 'Once, Jimmy, I might well have chafed, when I was a prairie-galloping hunter. Now, having gained a minute measure of enlightenment, I see that these annoyances of the flesh are no more significant than we allow them to be. Indeed, we can turn them to good use. Austerities are valuable. As for long delays, why, they are opportunities for study or, better yet, meditation. I have even learned to ignore spectators, and am grateful for the discipline which that forced me to acquire.'

We may be used to extraterrestrials these days. Nevertheless, he was the one Wodenite on this planet. And you take a being like that: four hoofed legs supporting a spike-backed, green-scaled, golden-bellied body and tail; torso, with arms in proportion, rising two meters to a crocodilian face, fangs, rubbery lips, bony ears, wistful brown eyes – you take that fellow and set him on a campus, in his equivalent of the lotus position, droning *'Om mani padme hum'* in a rich basso profundo, and see if you don't draw a crowd.

Serious though he was, Adzel never became a prig. He enjoyed good food and drink when he could get them, being especially fond of rye whiskey consumed out of beer tankards. He played murderous chess and poker. He sang, and sang well, everything from his native chants through human folk ballads on to the very latest spinnies. (A few things, such as *Eskimo Nell*, he refused to render in Betty's presence. From his avid reading of human history, he'd picked up anachronistic inhibitions.) I imagine his jokes often escaped me by being too subtle.

All in all, I was tremendously fond of him, hated the thought of his poverty, and had failed to hit on any way of helping him out.

I set my car down on the strip before his hut. A moldering conurb, black against feverish reflections off thickening fog, cast it into deep and sulfurous shadow. Unmuffled industrial traffic brawled around. I took a stun pistol from a drawer before escorting Betty outside.

Adzel's doorplate was kaput, but he opened at our knock. 'Do come in, do come in,' he greeted. Fluorolight shimmered gorgeous along his scales and scutes. Incense puffed outward. He noticed my gun. 'Why are you armed, Jimmy?'

'The night's dark here,' I said. 'In a crime area like this – '

'Is it?' He was surprised. 'Why, I have never been molested.'

We entered. He waved us to mats on the floor. Those, and a couple of cheap tables, and bookshelves cobbled together from scrap and crammed with codexes as well as reels, were his furniture. An Old Japanese screen – repro, of course – hid that end of the single room which contained a miniature cooker and some complicated specially installed plumbing. Two scrolls hung on the walls, one showing a landscape and one the Compassionate Buddha.

Adzel bustled about, making tea for us. He hadn't quite been able to adjust to these narrow surroundings. Twice I had to duck fast before his tail clonked me. (I said nothing, lest he spend the next half-hour in apologies.) 'I am delighted to see you,' he boomed. 'I gathered, however, from your call, that the occasion is not altogether happy.'

'We hoped you'd help us relax,' Betty replied. I myself felt a bit disgruntled. Sure, Adzel was fine people; but couldn't Betty and I relax in each other's company? I had seen too little of her these past weeks.

He served us. His pot held five liters, but – thanks maybe to that course in micrometrics – he could handle the tiniest cups and put on an expert tea ceremony. Appropriate silence passed. I fumed. Charming the custom might be; still, hadn't Oriental traditions caused me ample woe?

At last he dialled for *pipa* music, settled down before us on hocks and front knees, and invited: 'Share your troubles, dear friends.'

'Oh, we've been over them and over them,' Betty said. 'I came here for peace.'

'Why, certainly,' Adzel answered. 'I am glad to try to oblige. Would you like to join me in a spot of transcendental meditation?'

That tore my patience apart. 'No!' I yelled. They both stared at me. 'I'm sorry,' I mumbled. 'But . . . chaos, everything's gone bad and –'

A gigantic four-digited hand squeezed my shoulder, gently as my mother might have done. 'Tell, Jimmy,' Adzel said low.

It flooded from me, the whole sad, ludicrous situation. 'Freeman Snyder can't understand,' I finished. 'He thinks I can learn those equations, those facts, in a few days at most.'

'Can't you? Operant conditioning, for example –'

'You know better. I can learn to parrot, sure. But I won't get the knowledge down in my bones where it belongs. And they'll set me problems which require original thinking. They must. How else can they tell if I'll be able to handle an emergency in space?'

'Or on a new planet.' The long head nodded. 'Yes-s-s.'

'That's not for me,' I said flatly. 'I'll never be tagged by the merchant adventurers.' Betty squeezed my hand. 'Even freighters can run into grief, though.'

He regarded me for a while, most steadily, until at last he rumbled: 'A word to the right men – that does appear to be how your Technic civilization operates, no? *Zothkh.* Have you prospects for a quick performance of this task, that will allow you to get back soon to your proper work?'

'No. Freeman Snyder mentioned a float or display. Well, I'll have to soak up cultural background, and develop a scheme, and clear it with a local committee, and design the thing – which had better be spectacular as well as ethnic – and build it, and test it, and find the bugs in the design, and rebuild it, and – And I'm no artist anyhow. No matter how clever a machine I make, it won't look like much.'

Suddenly Betty exclaimed: 'Adzel, you know more about Old Oriental things than he does! Can't you make a suggestion?'

'Perhaps. Perhaps.' The Wodenite rubbed his jaw, a sandpaper noise. 'The motifs – Let me see.' He hooked a book off a shelf and started leafing through it. 'They are generally of pagan origin in Buddhistic, or for that matter Christian art . . . *Gr-r-rrr'm* . . . Betty, my sweet, while I search, won't you unburden yourself too?'

She twisted her fingers and gazed at the floor. I figured she'd rather not be distracted. Rising from my mat, I went to look over his shoulder – no, his elbow.

'My problem is my father's, actually,' she began. 'And maybe he and I already have solved it. That depends on whether or not one of the possibilities we've found is acceptable. If not – how much further can we research? Time's getting so short. He needs time to assemble a cast, rehearse, handle the physical details–' She noticed Adzel's puzzlement and managed a sort of chuckle. 'Excuse me. I got ahead of my story. We – '

'Hoy!' I interrupted. My hand slapped down on a page. 'What's that? . . . Uh, sorry, Betty.'

Her smile forgave me. 'Have you found something?' She sprang to her feet.

'I don't know,' I stammered, 'b-b-but, Adzel, that thing in this picture could almost be you. What is it?'

He squinted at the ideograms. 'The *lung*,' he said.

'A dragon?'

'Western writers miscalled it thus.' Adzel settled happily down to lecture us. 'The dragon proper was a creature of European and Near Eastern mythology, almost always a destructive monster. In Chinese and related societies, contrariwise, these herpetoids represented beneficent powers. The *lung* inhabited the sky, the *li* the ocean, the *chiao* the marshes and mountains. Various other entities are named elsewhere. The *lung* was the principal type, the one which was mimed on ceremonial occasions – '

The phone warbled. 'Would you please take that, Betty?' Adzel asked, reluctant to break off. 'I daresay it's a notification I am expecting of a change in class schedules. Now, Jimmy, observe the claws on hind and forefeet. Their exact number is a distinguishing characteristic of – '

'Dad!' Betty cried. Glancing sideways, I saw John Riefenstahl's mild features in the screen, altogether woebegon.

'I was hoping I'd find you, dear,' he said wearily. I knew that these days she seldom left the place without recording a list of numbers where she could probably be reached.

'I've just finished a three-hour conference with the board chairman,' her father's voice plodded. 'They've vetoed every one of our proposals.'

'Already?' she whispered. 'In God's name, why?'

'Various reasons. They feel *Carmen* is too parochial in time and space; hardly anybody today would understand what motivates the characters. *Alpha of the Centaur* is about space travel, which is precisely what we're supposed to get away from. *La Traviata* isn't visual enough. *Götterdämmerung*, they agree, has the Mythic Significance they want, but it's *too* visual. A modern audience wouldn't accept it unless we supply a realism of effects which would draw attention away from the live performers on whom it ought to center in a production that emphasizes Man. Et cetera, et cetera.'

'They're full of nonsense!'

'They're also full of power, dear. Can you bear to run through more tapes?'

'I'd better.'

'I beg your pardon, Freeman Riefenstahl,' Adzel put in. 'We haven't met but I have long admired your work. May I ask if you have considered Chinese opera?'

'The Chinese themselves will be doing that, Freeman – er – ' The conductor hesitated.

'Adzel.' My friend moved into scanner range. His teeth gleamed alarmingly sharp. 'Honored to make your acquaintance, sir . . . ah . . . sir?'

John Riefenstahl, who had gasped and gone bloodless, wiped

68

his forehead. 'Eh-eh-excuse me,' he stuttered. 'I didn't realize you – That is, here I had Wagner on my mind, and then Fafner himself confronted me –'

I didn't know those names, but the context was obvious. All at once Betty and I met each other's eyes and let out a yell.

Knowing how Simon Snyder would react, I insisted on a live interview. He sat behind his desk, surrounded by his computers, communicators, and information retrievers, and gave me a tight smile.

'Well,' he said. 'You have an idea, Jim? Overnight seems a small time for a matter this important.'

'It was plenty,' I answered. 'We've contacted the head of the Chinese-American committee, and he likes our notion. But since it's on behalf of the schools, he wants your okay.'

' "We"?' My counselor frowned. 'You have a partner?'

'Chaos, sir, he *is* my project. What's a Chinese parade without a dragon? And what fake dragon can possibly be as good as a live one? Now we take this Wodenite, and just give him a wig and false whiskers, claws over his hoofs, lacquer on his scales –'

'A nonhuman?' The frown turned into a scowl. 'Jim, you disappoint me. You disappoint me sorely. I expected better from you, some dedication, some application of your talents. In a festival devoted to your race, you want to feature an alien! No, I'm afraid I cannot agree –'

'Sir, please wait till you've met Adzel.' I jumped from my chair, palmed the hall door, and called: 'C'mon in.'

He did, meter after meter of him, till the office was full of scales, tail, spikes, and fangs. He seized Snyder's hand in a gentle but engulfing grip, beamed straight into Snyder's face, and thundered: 'How joyful I am at this opportunity, sir! What a way to express my admiration for terrestrial culture, and thus help glorify your remarkable species!'

'Um, well, that is,' the man said feebly.

I had told Adzel that there was no reason to mention his being a pacifist. He continued: 'I do hope you will approve Jimmy's brilliant idea, sir. To be quite frank, my motives are not unmixed. If I perform, I understand that the local restaurateurs' association will feed me during rehearsals. My stipend is exiguous and – ' he licked his lips, two centimeters from Snyder's nose – 'sometimes I get *so* hungry.'

He would tell only the strict, if not always the whole truth. I, having fewer compunctions, whispered in my counselor's ear: 'He is kind of excitable, but he's perfectly safe if nobody frustrates him.'

'Well.' Snyder coughed, backed away till he ran into a computer, and coughed again. 'Well. Ah . . . yes. Yes, Jim, your concept is undeniably original. There is a – ' he winced but got the words out – 'a certain quality to it which suggests that you – ' he strangled for a moment – 'will go far in life.'

'You plan to record that opinion, do you not?' Adzel asked. 'In Jimmy's permanent file? At once?'

I hurried them both through the remaining motions. My friend, my girl, and her father, had an appointment with the chairman of the board of the San Francisco Opera Company.

The parade went off like rockets. Our delighted local merchants decided to revive permanently the ancient custom of celebrating the Lunar New Year. Adzel will star in that as long as he remains on Earth. In exchange – since he brings in more tourist credits than it costs – he has an unlimited meal ticket at the Silver Dragon Chinese Food and Chop Suey Palace.

More significant was the production of Richard Wagner's *Siegfried*. At least, in his speech at the farewell performance, the governor of the Integrate said it was significant. 'Besides the bringing back of a musical masterpiece too many centuries neglected,' he pomped, 'the genius of John Riefenstahl has, by his choice of cast, given the Festival of Man an added dimension. He has reminded us that, in seeking our roots and pride, we must never grow chauvinistic. We must always remember to reach forth the hand of friendship to our brother beings throughout God's universe,' who might otherwise be less anxious to come spend their money on Earth.

The point does have its idealistic appeal, though. Besides, the show was a sensation in its own right. For years to come, probably, the complete Ring cycle will be presented here and there around the Commonwealth; and Freeman Riefenstahl can be guest conductor, and Adzel can sing Fafner, at top salary, any time they wish.

I won't see the end of that, because I won't be around. When everything had been settled, Adzel, Betty, and I threw ourselves a giant feast in his new apartment. After his fifth magnum of champagne, he gazed a trifle blurrily across the table and said to me:

'Jimmy, my affection for you, my earnest wish to make a fractional return of your kindness, has hitherto been baffled.'

'Aw, nothing to mention,' I mumbled while he stopped a volcanic hiccough.

'At any rate.' Adzel wagged a huge finger. 'He would be a poor friend who gave a dangerous gift.' He popped another cork and refilled our glasses and his stein. 'That is, Jimmy, I was aware of your ambition to get into deep space, and not as a plyer of routine routes but as a discoverer, a pioneer. The question remained, could you cope with unpredictable environments?'

I gaped at him. The heart banged in my breast. Betty caught my hand.

'You have convinced me you can,' Adzel said. 'True, Freeman Snyder may not give you his most ardent recommendation to the Academy. No matter. The cleverness and, yes, toughness with which you handled this problem – those convinced me, Jimmy, you are a true survivor type.'

He knocked back half a liter before tying the star-spangled bow knot on his package: 'Being here on a League scholarship, I have League connections. I have been in correspondence. A certain Master Merchant I know will soon be in the market for another apprentice and accepts what I have told him about you. Are you interested?'

I collapsed into Betty's arms. She says she'll find a way to follow me.

Too many of us unthinkingly think of David Falkayn as if he flashed into being upon Avalon like a lightning bolt. The Polesotechnic League we know of only in its decadence and downfall. Yet for long and long it was wing and talon of that Technic civilization which humans begot and from which many other races – Ythrians too, Ythrians too – drew fresh blood that still flows within them.

Remote from the centers of Technic might, unaccustomed to the idea that alien sophonts are alien in more than body, our ancestors in the first lifetimes after the Discovery were little aware of anything behind the occasional merchant vessels, scientists, hired teachers and consultants, that came to their planet. The complexity of roots, trunks, boughs, which upbore the leaf-crown they saw, lay beyond their ken. Even the visits of a few to Terra brought scant enlightenment.

Later ancestors, moving vigorously into space on their own, were better informed. Paradoxically, though, they had less to do with the League. By then they required no imports to continue development. Furthermore, being close to the stars in this sector, they competed so successfully for trade that League members largely withdrew from a region which had never been highly profitable for them. The main point of contact was the planet Esperance and it, being as yet thinly settled, was not a market which drew great flocks from either side.

Thus the ordinary Ythrian, up to this very year, has had only a footgrip upon reality where the League is concerned. He/she/youngling must strengthen this if the origins of the Avalonian

72

colony are to be made clear. What winds did Falkayn ride, what storms blew him hitherward at last?

His biographies tell how he became a protégé of Nicholas van Rijn, but say little about that merchant lord. You may well be surprised to learn that on numerous other worlds, it is the latter who lives in folk memory, whether as hero or rogue. He did truthfully fly in the front echelon of events when several things happened whose thunders would echo through centuries. With him as our archetype, we can approach knowledge.

Though hardly ever read or played anymore upon this globe, a good many accounts of him exist in Library Central, straightforward, semifictional, or romantic. Maychance the best introduction is the story which follows, from *Tales of the Great Frontier* by A. A. Craig.

MARGIN OF PROFIT

It was an anachronism to have a human receptionist in this hall of lucent plastic, among machines that winked and talked between jade columns soaring up into vaulted dimness – but a remarkably pleasant one when she was as long-legged and red-headed a stunblast as the girl behind the desk. Captain Torres drew to a crisp halt and identified himself. Traveling down sumptuous curves, his glance was jarred by the needle gun at her waist.

'Good day, sir,' she smiled. 'I'll see if Freeman van Rijn is ready for you.' She switched on an intercom. A three-megavolt oath bounced out. 'No, he's still in conference on the audivid. Won't you be seated?'

Before she turned the intercom off, Torres caught a few words: ' – he'll give us the exclusive franchise or we embargo, *ja*, and maybe arrange a little blockade too. Who in Satan's squatpot do these emperors on a single planet think they are? Hokay, he has a million soldiers under arms. You go tell him to take those soldiers, with hobnailed boots and rifles at port, and stuff them –' *Click.*

Torres wrapped cape around tunic and sat down, laying one polished boot across the other knee of his white culottes. He felt awkward, simultaneously overdressed and naked. The formal garb of a Lodgemaster in the Federated Brotherhood of Space-farers was a far removed from the coverall he wore in his ship or the loungers of groundside leave. And the guards in the lobby, a kilometer below, had not only checked his credentials and retinal patterns, they had made him deposit his sidearm.

Damn Nicholas van Rijn and the whole Polesotechnic

League! Good saints, drop him on Pluto with no underwear!

Of course, a merchant prince did have to be wary of kidnappers and assassins, though van Rijn himself was said to be murderously fast with a handgun. Nevertheless, arming your receptionist was not a polite thing to do.

Torres wondered, a trifle wistfully, if she was among the old devil's mistresses. Perhaps not. However, given the present friction between the Company – by extension, the entire League – and the Brotherhood, she'd have no time for him; her contract doubtless had a personal fealty clause. His gaze went to the League emblem on the wall behind her, a golden sunburst afire with jewels, surrounding an ancient rocketship, and the motto: *All the traffic will bear.* That could be taken two ways, he reflected sourly. Beneath it was the trademark of this outfit, the Solar Spice & Liquors Company.

The girl turned the intercom back on and heard only a steady rumble of obscenities. 'You may go in now, please,' she said, and to the speaker: 'Lodgemaster Captain Torres, sir, here for his appointment.'

The spaceman rose and passed through the inner door. His lean dark features were taut. This would be a new experience, meeting his ultimate boss. It was ten years since he had had to call anybody 'sir' or 'madam'.

The office was big, an entire side transparent, overlooking a precipitous vista of Djakarta's towers, green landscape hot with tropical gardens, and the molten glitter of the Java Sea. The other walls were lined with the biggest datacom Torres had ever seen, with shelves of extraterrestrial curios, and, astonishingly, a thousand or more codex-type books whose fine leather bindings showed signs of wear. Despite its expanse, the desktop was littered, close to maximum entropy. The most noticeable object on it was a small image of St Dismas, carved from Martian sandroot. Ventilators could not quite dismiss a haze and reek of tobacco smoke.

The newcomer snapped a salute. 'Lodgemaster Captain Torres speaking for the Brotherhood. Good day, sir.'

Van Rijn grunted. He was a huge man, two meters in height and more than broad enough to match. A triple chin and swag belly did not make him appear soft. Rings glittered on hairy

75

fingers and bracelets on brawny wrists, under snuff-soiled lace. Small black eyes, set close to a great hook nose under a sloping forehead, peered with laser intensity. He continued filling his pipe and said nothing until he had a good head of steam up.

'So,' he growled then, basso profundo, in an accent as thick as himself. 'You speak for the whole unspeakable union, I hope. Women members too? I have never understood why they want to say they belong to a brotherhood.' Waxed mustaches and long goatee waggled above a gorgeously embroidered waistcoat. Beneath it was only a sarong, which gave way to columnar ankles and bare splay feet.

Torres checked his temper. 'Yes, sir. Privately, informally, of course . . . thus far. I have the honor to represent all locals in the Commonwealth, and lodges outside the Solar System have expressed solidarity. We assume you will be a spokesman for the master merchants of the League.'

'In a subliminary way. I will shovel your demands along at my associates, what of them as don't hide too good in their offices and harems. Sit.'

Torres gave the chair no opportunity to mold itself to him. Perched on the edge, he proceeded harshly: 'The issue is very simple. The votes are now in, and the result can't surprise you. We are not calling a strike, you realize. But contracts or no, we will not take any more ships through the Kossaluth of Borthu until that menace has been ended. Any owner who tries to hold us to the articles and send us there will be struck. The idea of our meeting today, Freeman van Rijn, is to make that clear and get the League's agreement, without a lot of public noise that might bring on a real fight.'

'By damn, you cut your own throats like with a butterknife, slow and outscruciating.' The merchant's tone was surprisingly mild. 'Not alone the loss of pay and commissions. No, but if Sector Antares as not kept steady supplied, it loses taste maybe for cinnamon and London dry gin. Nor can other companies be phlegmatic about what they hawk. Like if Jo-Boy Technical Services bring in no more engineers and scientists, the colonies will train up their own. Hell's poxy belles! In a few years, no more market on any planet in those parts. You lose, I lose, we all lose.'

'The answer is obvious, sir. We detour around the Kossaluth. I know that'll take us through more hazardous regions, astronomically speaking, unless we go very far aside indeed. However, the brothers and sisters will accept either choice.'

'What?' Somehow van Rijn managed a bass scream. 'Is you developed feedback of the bowels? Double or quadruple the length of the voyage! Boost heaven-high the salaries, capital goods losses, survivors' compensation, insurance! Halve or quarter the deliveries per year! We are ruined! Better we give up Antares at once!'

The route was already expensive, Torres knew. He wasn't sure whether or not the companies could afford the extra cost; their books were their own secret. Having waited out the dramatics, he said patiently:

'The Borthudian press gangs have been operating for two years now, you know. Nothing that's been tried has stopped them. We have not panicked. If it had been up to the siblings at large, we'd have voted right at the start to bypass that horror-hole. But the Lodgemasters held back, hoping something could be worked out. Apparently that isn't possible.'

'See here,' van Rijn urged. 'I don't like this no better than you. Worse, maybe. The losses my company alone has took could make me weep snot. We can afford it, though. Naked-barely, but we can. Figure it. About fifteen percent of our ships altogether gets captured. We would lose more, traveling through the Gamma Mist or the Stonefields. And those crews would not be prisoners that we are still working to have released. No, they would be kind of dead. As for making a still bigger roundabout through nice clear vacuum, well, that would be safe, but means an absolute loss on each run. Even if your brotherhood will take a big cut in the exorbital wages you draw, still, consider the tieup of bottom on voyages so long. We do have trade elsewheres to carry on.'

Torres' temper snapped across. 'Go flush your dirty financial calculations! Try thinking about human beings for once. We'll face meteroid swarms, infrasuns, rogue planets, black holes, radiation bursts, hostile natives – but have you *met* one of those impressed men? I have. That's what decided me, and made me take a lead in getting the Brotherhood to act. I'm not going to risk it happening to me, nor to any lodge sibling of mine. Why don't you and your fellow moneymen conn the ships personally?'

'Ho-o-o,' murmured van Rijn. He showed no offense, but leaned across the desk on his forearms. 'You tell me, ha?'

Torres must force the story out. 'Met him on Arkan III – on the fringe of the Kossaluth, autonomous planet, you recall. We'd put in with a consignment of tea. A ship of theirs was in too, and you can bet your brain we went around in armed parties, ready to shoot any Borthudian who might look like a crimp. Or any Borthudian at all; but they kept to themselves. Instead, I saw him, this man they'd snatched, going on some errand. I spoke to him. My friends and I even tried to capture him, so we could bring him back to Earth and get reversed what that electronic hell-machine had done to him – He fought us and got away. God! He'd've been more free if he were in chains. And still I could feel how he wanted out, he was screaming inside, but he couldn't break the conditioning *and he couldn't go crazy either* –'

Torres grew aware that van Rijn had come around the desk and was thrusting a bottle into his hand. 'Here, you drink some from this,' the merchant said. The liquor burned the whole way down. 'I have seen a conditioned man myself once, long ago when I was a rough-and-tumbler. A petty native prince had got it done to him, to keep him for a technical expert when he wanted to go home. We did catch him that time, and took him back for treatment.' He returned to his chair and rekindled his pipe. 'First, though, we got together with the ship's engineer and made us a little firecracker what we blew off at the royal palace.' He chuckled. 'The yield was about five kilotons.'

'If you want to outfit a punitive expedition, sir,' Torres rasped, 'I guarantee you can get full crews.'

'No.' Curled, shoulder-length black locks swished greasily as van Rijn shook his head. 'You know the League does not have much of a combat fleet. The trouble with capital ships is, they tie up capital. It is one thing to use a tiny bit of force on a planetbound lordling what has got unreasonable. It is another thing to take on somebody what can take you right on back. Simple tooling up for a war with Borthu, let alone fighting one,

78

would bring many members companies close to bankrupture.'

'But what about the precedent, if you tamely let these out-rages go on? Who'll be next to make prey of you?'

'*Ja*, there is that. But there is also the Commonwealth govern-ment. We try any big-size action, we traders, even though it is far outside the Solar System, and right away we get gibberings about our "imperialism". We could get lots of trouble made for us, right here in the heart of civilization. Maybe we get called pirates, because we is not a government ourselves with politicians and bureaucrats telling people what to do. Maybe Sol would actual-like intervene against us on behalf of the Kossaluth, what is "only exercising sovereignty within its legiti-mate sphere". You know how diplomats from Earth has not made any hard effort for getting Borthu to stop. In fact, I tell you, a lot of politicians feel quite chortlesome when they see us wicked profiteers receiving some shaftcraft.'

Torres stirred in his seat. 'Yes, of course, I'm as disgusted as you with the official reaction, or lack of reaction. But what about the League? I mean, its leaders must have been trying measures short of war. I take it those have come to naught.'

'You take that, boy, and keep it for yourself, because I for sure don't want it. *Ja*. Correct. Threats the Borthudians grin at, knowing how hard pinched we is and where. Not good trade offers nor economic sanctions has worked; they is not interested in trade with us. Rathermore, they do expect we will soon shun their territory, like you now want us to. That suits their masters well, not having foreign influentials . . . Bribes? How do you bribe a being what ranks big in his own civilization and species, both those alien to you? Assassins? *Ach*, I am afraid we squan-dered several good assassins for no philanthropic result.' Van Rijn cursed for two straight minutes without repeating himself. 'And there they sit, fat and greedy-gut, across the route to Antares and all stars beyond! It is not to be stood for! No, it is to be jumped on!'

Presently he finished in a calmer tone: 'This ultimatum of yours brings matters to a head. Speaking of heads, it is getting time for a tall cold beer. I will soon throw a little brainbooting session with a few fellows and see what oozes out. Maybe we can invent something. You go tell the crewmen they should sit bottom-tight for a while yet, *nie*? Now, would you like to join me in the bar? – No? Then good day to you, Captain, if possible.'

It is a truism that the structure of a society is basically determined by its technology. Not in an absolute sense – there may be totally different cultures using identical tools – but the tools settle the possibilities; you can't have interstellar trade without spaceships. A race limited to a single planet, possessing a high knowledge of mechanics but with its basic machines of industry and war requiring a large capital investment, will inevitably tend toward collectivism under one name or another. Free enterprise needs elbow room.

Automation and the mineral wealth of the Solar System made the manufacture of most goods cheap. The cost of energy nosedived when small, clean, simple fusion units became available. Gravitics led to the hyperdrive, which opened a galaxy to exploitation. This also provided a safety valve. A citizen who found his government oppressive could often emigrate elsewhere, an exodus – the Breakup, as it came to be called – that planted liberty on a number of worlds. Their influence in turn loosened bonds upon the mother planet.

Interstellar distances being what they are, and intelligent races having their separate ideas of culture, there was no political union of them. Nor was there much armed conflict; besides the risk of destruction, few had anything to fight about. A race rarely gets to be intelligent without an undue share of built-in ruthlessness, so all was not sweetness and fraternity. However, the various balances of power remained fairly stable. Meanwhile the demand for cargoes grew huge. Not only did colonies want the luxuries of home, and home want colonial products, but the older civilizations had much to swap. It was usually cheaper to import such things than to create the industry needed to make synthetics and substitutes.

Under such conditions, an exuberant capitalism was bound to arise. It was also bound to find mutual interests, form alliances, and negotiate spheres of influence. The powerful companies might be in competition, but their magnates had the wit to see that, overriding this, they shared a need to cooperate in many activities, arbitrate disputes among themselves, and present a united front to the demands of the state – any state.

Governments were limited to a few planetary systems at most; they could do little to control their cosmopolitan merchants. One by one, through bribery, coercion, or sheer despair, they gave up the struggle.

Selfishness is a potent force. Governments, officially dedicated to altruism, remained divided. The Polesotechnic League became a loose kind of supergovernment, sprawling from Canopus to Deneb, drawing is membership and employees from perhaps a thousand species. It was a horizontal society, cutting across political and cultural boundaries. It set its own policies, made its own treaties, established its own bases, fought its own battles . . . and for a time, in the course of milking the Milky Way, did more to spread a truly universal civilization and enforce a solid *Pax* than all the diplomats in known history.

Nevertheless, it had its troubles.

A mansion among those belonging to Nicholas van Rijn lay on the peak of Kilimanjaro, up among the undying snows. It was an easy spot to defend, just in case, and a favorite for conferences.

His car slanted down through a night of needle-sharp stars, toward high turrets and glowing lights. Looking through the canopy, he picked out Scorpio. Antares flashed a red promise. He shook his fist at the fainter, unseen suns between him and it. 'So!' he muttered. 'Monkey business with van Rijn. The whole Sagittarius direction waiting to be opened, and you in the way. By damn, this will cost you money, gut and kipper me if it don't.'

He thought back to days when he had ridden ships through yonder spaces, bargaining in strange cities or stranger wildernesses, or beneath unblue skies and in poisonous winds, for treasures Earth had not yet imagined. For a moment, wistfulness tugged at him. A long time now since he had been any further than the Moon . . . poor, aging fat man, chained to a single planet and cursed whenever he turned an honest credit. The Antares route was more important than he cared to admit

6   81

aloud. If he lost it, he lost his chance at the pioneering that went on beyond, to corporations with offices on the other side of the Kossaluth. You went on expanding or you went under, and being a conspicuous member of the League wouldn't save you. Of course, he could retire, but then what would there be to engage his energies?

The car landed itself. Household staff, liveried and be-weaponed, sprang to flank him as he emerged. He wheezed thin chill air into sooty lungs, drew his cloak of phosphorescent onthar skin tightly around him, and scrunched up a graveled garden path to the house. A new maid stood at the door, pert and pretty. He tossed his plumed cap at her and considered making a proposition, but the butler said that the invited persons were already here. Seating himself, more for show than because of weariness, he told the chair, 'Conference room' and rolled along corridors paneled in the woods of a dozen planets. A sweet smell of attar of janie and a softly played Mozart quintet enlivened the air.

Four colleagues were poised around a table when he entered, a datacom terminal before each. Kraaknach of the Martian Transport Company was glowing his yellow eyes at a Frans Hals on the wall. Firmage of North American Engineering registered impatience with a puffed cigar. Mjambo, who owned Jo-Boy Technical Services, was talking into his wristphone, but stopped when his host entered. Gornas-Kiew happened to be on Earth and was authorized to speak for the Centaurian con-glomerate; 'he' sat hunched into 'his' shell, naught moving save the delicate antennae.

Van Rijn plumped his mass into an armchair at the head of the table. Waiters appeared with trays of drinks, snacks, and smokes catered for the individuals present. He took a large bite from a limburger-and-onion sandwich and looked inquiringly at the rest.

Kraaknach's face, owlish within the air helmet, turned to him. 'Well, Freeman who receives us,' he trilled and croaked, 'I understand we are met on account of this Borthudian *hrokna.* Did the spacemen make their expected demand?'

'*Ja.*' Van Rijn chose a cigar and rolled it between his fingers. 'The situation is changed from desperate to serious. They will

82

not take ships through the Kossaluth, except to fight, while this shanghai business goes on.'

'I suppose it is quite unfeasible to deliver a few gigatons' worth of warhead at the Borthudian home planet?' asked Mjambo.

Van Rijn tugged his goatee. 'Death and damnation!' He checked his temper. After all, he had invited these specific sophonts here precisely because they had not yet been much concerned with the problem. It had affected their enterprises in varying degrees, of course, but interests elsewhere had been tying up their direct attention. This tiny, outlying corner of the galaxy which Technic civilization has slightly explored is that big and various. Van Rijn was hoping for a fresh viewpoint.

Having repeated the objections he had given Torres, he added: 'I must got to admit, also, supposing we could, slaughtering several billion sentients because their leaders make trouble for us is not nice. I do not think the League would long survive being so guilty. Besides, it is wasteful. They should better be made customers of ours.'

'Limited action, whittling down their naval strength till they see reason?' wondered Firmage.

'I have had more such programs run through the computers than there is politicians in hell,' van Rijn answered. 'They every one give the same grismal answer. Allowing for minimal losses, compensations, salaries, risk bonuses, construction, maintenance, replacement, ammunition, depreciation, loss of business due to lack of supervision elsewhere, legal action brought by the Solar Commonwealth and maybe other governments, bribes, loss of profit if the money was invested where it ought to be, et bloody-bestonkered cetera . . . in a nutshell, we cannot afford it.' Reminded, he told the butler, 'Simmons, you gluefoot, a bowl of mixed-up nuts, chop-chop, only you don't chop them, understand?'

'You will pardon my ignorance, good sirs,' clicked Gornas-Kiew's vocalizer. 'I have been quite marginally aware of this unpleasantness. Why are the Borthudians impressing human crews?'

Firmage and Mjambo stared. They had known Centaurians are apt to be single-minded – but this much? Van Rijn simply

83

cracked a Brazil nut between his teeth, awing everybody present except for Gornas-Kiew, and reached for a snifter of brandy. 'The gruntbrains have not enough of their own,' he said.

'Perhaps I can make it clear,' said Kraaknach. Like many Martians of the Sirruch Horde – the latest wave of immigrants to Earth's once desolate neighbor – he was a natural-hatched lecturer. He ran a clawed hand across gray feathers, stuck a rinn tube through the intake sphincter on his helmet, and lit it.

'Borthu is a backward planet, terrestoid to eight points, with autochthons describable as humanoid,' he began. 'They were at an early industrial, nuclear-power stage when explorers visited them, and their reaction to the presence of a superior culture was paranoid. At least, it was in the largest nation, which shortly proceeded to conquer the rest. It had modernized technologically with extreme rapidity, aided by certain irresponsible elements of this civilization who helped it for high pay. United, the Borthudians set out to acquire an interstellar empire. Today they dominate a space about forty light-years across, though they actually occupy just a few Solar-type systems within it. By and large, they want nothing to do with the outside universe: doubtless because the rulers fear that such contact will be dangerous to the stability of their régime. Certainly they are quite able to supply their needs within the boundaries of their dominion – with the sole exception of efficient spacemen. If we ourselves, with all our capabilities in the field of robotics, have not yet been able to produce totally automated spacecraft which are reliable, how much worse must the Borthudians feel the lack of enough crews.'

'Hm,' said Firmage. 'I've already thought about subversion. I can't believe their whole populace is happy. If we could get only a few regularly scheduled freighters in there . . . double agents . . . the Kossalu and his whole filthy government overthrown from within –'

'Of course we will follow that course in due course, if we can,' van Rijn interrupted. 'But at best it takes much time. Meanwhile, competitors sew up the Sagittarius frontier. We need a *quick* way to get back our routes through that space.'

Kraaknach puffed oily smoke. 'To continue,' he said, 'the Borthudians can build as many ships as they wish, which is a

84

great many since their economy is expanding. In fact, that economy requires constant expansion if the whole empire is not to collapse, inasmuch as the race-mystique of its masters has promoted a population explosion. But they cannot produce trained spacehands at the needful rate. Pride, and a not unjustified fear of ideological contamination, prevents them from sending students to Technic planets, or hiring from among us; and they have only one understaffed astronautical academy of their own.'

'I know,' said Mjambo. 'It'd be a whopping good market for me if we could change their minds for them.'

'Accordingly,' Kraaknach proceeded, 'they have in the past two years taken to waylaying our vessels. Doubtless they expect to be shunned eventually, as the Brotherhood has now voted to do. But then they can afford to let much of their population die back, while using what manned ships they have to maintain the rest. Without fear of direct or indirect interference from outside, the masters can "remold" Borthudian society at leisure. It is a pattern not unknown to Terrestrial history, I believe.

'At present, their actions are obviously in defiance of what has been considered interstellar law. However, only the Commonwealth, among government, has the potential of doing anything about it – and there is such popular revulsion on Earth at the thought of war that the Commonwealth has confined itself to a few feeble protests. Indeed, a strong faction in it is not displeased to see the arrogant Polesotechnic League discomfited. Certain spokesmen are even arguing that territorial sovereignty should be formally recognized as extending through interstellar space. A vicious principle if ever there was one, *hru*?'

He extracted the rinn tube and dropped it down an ashtaker. 'In any event,' he finished, 'they capture the men, brain-channel them, and assign them to their own transport fleet. It takes years to train an astronaut. We are losing a major asset in this alone.'

'Can't we improve our evasive action?' inquired Firmage. 'Any astronomical distance is so *damn* big. Why can't we avoid their patrols altogether?'

'Eighty-five percent of our ships do precisely that,' van Rijn reminded him. 'It is not enough. The unlucky minority – '

85

– who were detected by sensitive instruments within the maximum range of about a light-year, by the instantaneous pseudogravitational pulses of hyperdrive; on whom the Borthudians then closed in, using naval vessels which were faster and more maneuverable than merchantmen –

'– they is gotten to be too many by now. The Brotherhood will accept no more. Confidential amongst the we of us, I would not either. And, *ja*, plenty different escape tactics is been tried, as well as cutting engines and lying low. None of them work very good.'

'Well, then, how about convoying our ships through?' Firmage persisted.

'At what cost? I have been with the figures. It also would mean operating the Antares run at a loss – quite apart from those extra warcraft we would have to build. It would make Sagittarian trade out of the damned question.'

'Why can't we arm the merchantmen themselves?'

'Bah! Wasn't you listening to Freeman Kraaknach? Robotics is never yet got to where live brains can be altogether replaced, except in bureaucrats.' Deliberately irritating, which might pique forth ideas, van Rijn added what was everybody's knowledge:

'A frigate-class ship needs twenty men for the weapons and instruments. An unarmed freighter needs only four. Consider the wages paid to spacefolk; we would really get folked. Also, sixteen extra on every ship would mean cutting down operations elsewhere, for lack of crews. Not to mention the cost of the outfitting. We cannot afford all this; we would lose money in big fat globs. What is worse, the Kossalu knows we would. He need only wait, holding back his fig-plucking patrols, till we is too broke to continue. Then he would maybe be tempted to start conquering some more, around Antares.'

Firmage tapped the table with a restless finger. 'Everything we've thought of seems to be ruled out,' he said. 'Suggestions, anybody?'

Silence grew, under the radiant ceiling.

Gornas-Kiew broke it: 'Precisely how are captures made? It is impossible to exchange shots while in hyperdrive.'

'Statistically impossible,' amended Kraaknach. 'Energy beams are out of the question. Material missiles have to be hypered themselves, or they would revert to true, sublight velocity and be left behind as soon as they emerged from the drive field. Furthermore, to make a hit, they must be precisely in phase with the target. A good pilot can phase in on another ship, but the operation involves too many variables for any cybernet of useful size.'

'I tell you how,' snarled van Rijn. 'The pest-bedamned Borthudians detect the vibration-wake from afar. They compute an intercept course. Coming close, they phase in and slap on a tractor beam. Then they haul themselves up alongside, burn through the hull or an airlock, and board.'

'Why, the answer looks simple enough,' said Mjambo. 'Equip our craft with pressor beams. Keep the enemy ships at arm's length.'

'You forget, esteemed colleague, that beams of either positive or negative sign are powered from the engine,' said Kraaknach. 'A naval vessel has much stronger engines than a merchantman.'

'Give our crews small arms. Let them blast down the boarding parties.'

'The illegitimate-offspring-of-interspecies-crosses Borthudians already have arms, also hands what hold weapons,' snorted van Rijn. 'Phosphor and farts! Do you think four men can stand off twenty?'

'M-m-m . . . yes, I see your point.' Firmage nodded. 'But look here, we can't do anything about this without laying out *some* cash. I'm not sure what the mean profit is –'

'On the average, for everybody's combined Antarean voyages, about thirty percent on each run,' said van Rijn promptly.

Mjambo started. 'How the devil do you get figures for my company?' he exclaimed.

Van Rijn grinned and drew on his cigar.

'That gives us a margin to use,' said Gornas-Kiew. 'We can invest in military equipment to such an extent that our profit is less – though I agree there must still be a final result in the black – for the duration of this emergency.'

'It'd be worth it,' said Mjambo. 'In fact, I'd take a fair-sized loss just to teach those bastards a lesson.'

'No, no.' Van Rijn lifted a hand which, after years in offices, was still the broad muscular paw of a working spaceman. 'Revenge and destruction are un-Christian thoughts. Also, I have told you, they do not pay very well, since it is hard to sell anything to a corpse. The problem is to find some means inside our resources what will make it unprofitable for Borthu to raid us. Not being stupid heads, they will then stop raiding and we can maybe later do business.'

'You're a cold-blooded one,' said Mjambo.

'Not always,' replied van Rijn blandly. 'Like a sensible man, I set my thermostat according to what is called for. In this case, what we need is a scientifical approach with elegant mathematics – '

Abruptly he dropped his glance and covered a shiver by pouring himself another glassful. He had gotten an idea.

When the others had argued for a fruitless hour, he said: 'Freeman, this gets us nowhere, *nie*? Perhaps we are not stimulated enough to think clear.'

'What do you propose?' sighed Mjambo.

'Oh . . . an agreement. A pool, or prize, or reward for whoever solves this problem. For example, ten percent of everybody else's Antarean profits for the next ten years.'

'Hoy, there!' burst from Firmage. 'If I know you, you robber, you've come up with an answer.'

'No, no, no. By my honor I swear it. I have some beginning thoughts, maybe, but I am only a poor rough old space walloper without the fine education you beings have had. I could too easy be wrong.'

'What is your notion?'

'Best I not say yet, until it is more fermented. But please to note, he who tries something active will take on the risk and expense. If he succeeds, he save profits for all. Does not a tiny return on his investment sound fair and proper?'

There was more argument. Van Rijn smiled with infinite benevolence. He settled at last for a compact, recorded on ciphertape, whose details would be computed later.

Beaming, he clapped his hands. 'Freemen,' he said, 'we have worked hard tonight and soon comes much harder work. By damn, I think we deserve a little celebration. Simmons, prepare an orgy.'

Rafael Torres had considered himself unshockable by any mere words. He was wrong. 'Are you serious?' he gasped.

'In confidentials, of course,' van Rijn answered. 'The crew must be good men like you. Can you recommend more?'

'No —'

'We will not be stingy with the bonuses.'

Torres shook his head violently. 'Out of the question, sir. The Brotherhood's refusal to enter the Kossaluth on anything except a punitive expedition is absolute. This one you propose is not, as you describe it. We can't lift the ban without another vote, which would necessarily be a public matter.'

'You can publicly vote again after we see if the idea works,' van Rijn pressed him. 'The first trip will have to be secret.'

'Then the first trip will have to do without a crew.'

'Bile on a boomerang!' Van Rijn's fist crashed against his desk. He surged to his feet. 'What sort of putzing cowards do I deal with? In my day we were men! And we had ideals, I can tell you. We would have boosted through hell's open gates if you paid us enough.'

Torres sucked hard on his cigarette. 'The ban must stand. None but a Lodgemaster can — Well, all right, I'll say it.' Anger was a cold flaring in him. 'You want men to take an untried ship into enemy sky and invite attack. If they lose, they're condemned to a lifetime of praying, with what's left of their wills, for death. If they succeed, they win a few measly kilo-credits. In either case, you sit back here plump and safe. God damn it, no!'

Van Rijn stood quiet for a while. This was something he had not quite foreseen.

His gaze wandered forth, out the transparency, to the narrow sea. A yacht was passing by, lovely in white sails and slender hull. Really, he ought to spend more time on his own. Money wasn't that important. Was it? This was not such a bad world, this Earth, even when one was being invaded by age and fat. It was full of blossoms and burgundy, clean winds and lovely

women, Mozart melodies and fine books. Doubtless his
memories of earlier days in space were colored by nostalgia . . .

He reached a decision and turned around to face his visitor.
'A Lodgemaster can come on such a trip without telling
peoples,' he said. 'The union rules give you discretion. You
think you can raise two more like yourself, hah?'

'I told you, Freeman, I won't so much as consider it.'

'Even if I myself am the skipper?'

The *Mercury* did not, outwardly, look different after the engineers were finished with her. Her cargo was the same as usual,
too: cinnamon, ginger, pepper, cloves, tea, whisky, gin. If he
was going to Antares, van Rijn did not intend to waste the
voyage. He did omit wines, doubting their quality could stand
as rough a trip as this one would be.

The alterations were internal, extra hull bracing and a new
and monstrously powerful engine. The actuarial computers
estimated the cost of such an outfitting as three times the total
profit from all her journeys during an average service life. Van
Rijn had winced, but put a shipyard to work.

In truth, his margin was slim, and he was gambling more on
it than he could afford to lose. However, if the Kossalu of
Borthu had statisticians of his own – always assuming that the
idea proved out –

Well, if it didn't Nicholas van Rijn would die in battle, or be
liquidated as too old for usefulness, or become a brain-
channeled slave, or be held for a ruinous ransom. The possibilities looked about equally bad.

He installed himself, dark-haired and multiply curved Dorcas
Gherardini, and a stout supply of brandy, tobacco, and ripe
cheese, in the captain's cabin. One might as well be comfortable.
Torres was his mate, Captains Petrovich and Seiichi his
engineers. The *Mercury* lifted from Quito Spaceport without
fanfare, waited unpretentiously in orbit for clearance, then
accelerated on negagrav away from Sol. At the required distance, she went on hyperdrive and outpaced light.

Van Rijn sat back on the bridge and lit his churchwarden
pipe. 'Now is a month's going to Antares,' he said piously.
'Good St Dismas, watch over us.'

'I'll stick by St Nicholas, patron of travelers,' replied Torres. 'In spite of his being your namesake.'

Van Rijn looked hurt. 'By damn, do you not respect my morals?'

Torres shrugged. 'Well, I admire your courage – nobody can say you lack guts – ' van Rijn gave him a hard look – 'and if anybody can pull this off, you can. Set a pirate to catch a pirate.'

'You younger generations got a loud mouth and no manners.' The merchant blew malodorous clouds. 'In my day, we said "sir" to the captain even when we mutinied.'

'I'm still worried about a particular detail,' admitted Torres. He had had much more to occupy mind and body than the working out of strategies, mainly the accumulation of as many enjoyable memories as possible. 'I suppose it's a fairly safe bet that the enemy hasn't yet heard about our travel ban. Still, the recent absence of ships must have made him think. Besides, our course brings us so near a known Borthudian base that we're certain to be detected. Suppose he gets suspicious and dispatches half a dozen vessels to jump us?'

'The likelihood of that is quite low, because he keeps his bloody-be-damned patrol craft cruising far apart, to maximize their chances of spotting a catch. If he feels wary of us, he will simply not attack; but this also I doubt, for a prize is valuable.' Van Rijn heaved his bulk onto his feet. One good thing about spacefaring, you could set the gravity-field generator low and feel almost lissome again. 'What you at your cockamamie age do not quite understand, my friend, is that there are hardly any certainties in life. Always we must go on probabilities. The secret of success is to make the odds favor you. Then in the long run you are sure to come out ahead. It is your watch now, and I recommend you project a book on statistical theory to pass the time. The data bank has an excellent library. As for me, I will be in conference with Freelady Gherardini.'

'I wish to blazes I could run commands of mine the way you run this of yours,' said Torres mournfully.

Van Rijn waved an expansive hand. 'Why not, my boy, why not? So long as you make money and no trouble for the Company, the Company does not peek over your shoulder. The trouble with you young snapperwhippers is you lack initiative. When you are a poor old feeble fat man like me, you will look back and regret your lost opportunities.'

Low-gee or no, the deck thumped beneath his feet as he departed.

Heaven was darkness filled with a glory of suns. Viewscreens framed the spilling silver of the Milky Way, ruby spark of Antares, curling edge of a nebula limned by the glare of an enmeshed star. Brightest in vision stood Borthu's, yellow as minted gold.

The ship drove on as she had done for a pair of weeks, pulsing in and out of four-space at thousands of times per second, loaded with a tension that neared the detonation point.

On a wardroom bench, Dorcas posed slim legs and high prow with a care so practiced as to be unconscious. She could not pull her eyes from the screen. 'It's beautiful,' she said in a small voice. 'Somehow that doubles the horror.'

Van Rijn sprawled beside her, his majestic nose aimed aloft. 'What is horrible, my little sinusoid?' he asked.

'Them . . . waiting to pounce on us and – In God's name, why did I come along?'

'I believe there was mention of a tygron coat and flamedrop earrings.'

'But suppose they do capture us.' Cold, her fingers clutched at his arm. 'What will happen to me?'

'I told you I have set up a ransom fund for you. I told you also, maybe they will not bother to collect it, or maybe we get broken to bits in the fight. Satan's horn and the devil who gave them to him! Be still, will you?'

The audio intercom came to life with Torres' urgent words: 'Wake of high-powered ship detected, approaching to intercept.'

'All hands to stations!' roared van Rijn.

Dorcas screamed. He tucked her under one arm, carried her down the passageway – collecting a few scratches en route – to his cabin, where he tossed her on the bed and told her she'd better strap in. Puffing, he arrived on the bridge. The visuals showed Petrovich and Seiichi in the engine room, armored, their faces a-glisten with sweat. Torres sat gnawing his lip, fingers unsteady as he tuned instruments.

'Hokay,' said van Rijn, 'here is the thing we have come for. I hope you each remember what you have to do, because this is not another rehearsal where I can gently correct your thumb-brained mistakes. He whacked his great bottom into the main control chair and secured the safety harness. When his fingers tickled the console, giving computers and efferent circuits their orders, he felt the sensitive response of that entire organism which was the ship. Thus far *Mercury* had been under normal power, the energy generator half-idle. It was good to know how many wild horses he could call up.

The strange vessel drew in communication range, where the two drive fields measurably impinged on each other. As customary, both pilots felt their way toward the same phase and frequency of oscillation, until a radio wave could pass between them and be received. On the bridge of the human craft, the outercom chimed. Torres pressed the accept button and the screen came to life.

A Borthudian officer looked out. His garments clung dead black to a cat-lithe frame. The face was semihuman, though hairless and tinged with blue; yellow eyes smoldered under a narrow forehead. Behind him could be seen his own bridge, a companion who sat before a fire-control terminal, and the usual six-armed basalt idol.

'Terrestrial ship ahoy!' He ripped out fluent Anglic, harshly accented by the shapes of larynx and mouth. 'This is Captain Rentharik of the Kossalu's frigate *Gantok*. By the law, most sacred, of the Kossaluth of Borthu, you are guilty of trespass on the domains of His Mightiness. Stand by to be boarded.'

'Why, you out-from-under-wet-logs-crawling cockypop!' Van Rijn made himself flush turkey red. 'Not bad enough you hijack my men and transports, with their good expensive cargoes, but you have the copperbound nerve to call it legal!'

Rentharik fingered a small ceremonial dagger hung about his neck. 'Old man, the writ of the Kossalu runs through this entire volume of space. You can save yourself added punishment – nerve-pulsing – by submitting peacefully to judgment.'

'It is understood by *civilized* races that interstellar space is free for every innocent passage.'

Rentharik smiled, revealing bright-green teeth of nonhuman shape. 'We enforce our own laws here, Captain.'

'*Ja*, but by damn, this time you are trying to use force on van Rijn. They are going to be surprised back on that dingleberry you call your home planet.'

Rentharik spoke at a recorder in his native language. 'I have just made a note recommending you be assigned to the Ilyan run after conditioning. Organic compounds in the atmosphere there produce painful allergic reactions in your species, yet not so disabling that we consider it worthwhile to issue airsuits. Let the rest of your crew pay heed.'

Van Rijn's face lit up. 'Listen, if you would hire spacemen honest instead of enslaving them, we got plenty of antiallergenic treatments and medicines. I would be glad to supply you them, at quite a reasonable commission.'

'No more chatter. You are to be grappled and boarded. Captured personnel receive nerve-pulsing in proportion to the degree of their resistance.'

Rentharik's image blanked.

Torres licked sandy lips. Turning up the magnification in a viewscreen, he picked out the Borthudian frigate. She was a darkling shark-form, only half the tonnage of the dumpy merchantman but with gun turrets etched against remote star-clouds She came riding in along a smooth curve, matched hypervelocities with practiced grace, and flew parallel to her prey, a few kilometers off.

The intercom gave forth a scream. Van Rijn swore as the visual showed him Dorcas, out of her harness and raving around his cabin in utter hysterics. Why, she might spill all his remaining liquor, and Antares still eleven days off!

A small, pulsing jar went through hull and bones. *Gantok* had reached forth a tractor beam and laid hold of *Mercury*.

'Torres,' said van Rijn. 'You stand by, boy, and take over if somewhat happens to me. I maybe want your help anyway, if the game gets too gamy. Petrovich, Seiichi, you got to maintain our own beams and hold them tight, no matter what. Hokay? We go!'

Gantok was pulling herself closer. Petrovich kicked in full power. For a moment, safety arcs, blazed blue, ozone spat forth a smell of thunder, a roar filled the air. Then equilibrium was reached, with only a low droning to bespeak unthinkable energies at work.

A pressor beam lashed out, an invisible hammerblow of repulsion, five times the strength of the enemy tractor. Van Rijn heard *Mercury*'s ribs groan with the stress. *Gantok* shot away, turning end over end, until she was lost to vision among the stars.

'Ha, ha!' bellowed van Rijn. 'We spill their apples, eh? By damn! Next we show them real fun!'

The Borthudian hove back in sight. She clamped on again, full-strength attraction. Despite the pressor, *Mercury* was yanked toward her. Seiichi cursed and gave back his full thrust.

For a moment van Rijn thought his ship would burst open. He saw a deckplate buckle under his feet and heard metal elsewhere shear. But *Gantok* was batted away as if by a troll's fist.

'Not so hard! Not so hard, you dumbhead! Let me control the beams.' Van Rijn's hands danced over the console. 'We want to keep him for a souvenir, remember?'

He used a spurt of drive to overhaul the foe. His right hand steered *Mercury* while his left wielded the tractor and the pressor, seeking a balance. The engine noise rose to a sound like heavy surf. The interior gee-field could not compensate for all the violence of accelerations now going on; harness creaked as his weight was hurled against it. Torres, Petrovich, and Seiichi made themselves part of the machinery, additions to the computer systems which implemented the commands his fingers gave.

The Borthudian's image vanished out of viewscreens as he slipped *Mercury* into a different phase. Ordinarily this would have sundered every contact between the vessels. However, the gravitic forces which he had locked onto his opponent paid no heed to how she was oscillating between relativistic and nonrelativistic quantum states; her mass remained the same. He had simply made her weapons useless against him, unless her pilot matched his travel pattern again. To prevent that, he ordered a program of random variations, within feasible limits.

95

Given time to collect data, perform stochastic analysis, and exercise the intuition of a skilled living brain, the enemy pilot could still have matched; such a program could not be random in an absolute sense. Van Rijn did not propose to give him time.

Now thoroughly scared, the Borthudian opened full drive and tried to break away. Van Rijn equalized positive and negative forces in a heterodyning interplay which, in effect, welded him fast. Laughing, he threw his own superpowered engine into reverse. *Gantok* shuddered to a halt and went backwards with him. The fury of that made *Mercury* cry out in every member. He could not keep the linkage rigid without danger of being broken apart; he must vary it, flexibly, yet always shortening the gap between hulls.

'Ha, like a fish we play him! Good St Peter the Fisherman, help us not let him get away!'

Through the racket around him, van Rijn heard something snap, and felt a rushing of air. Petrovich cried it for him: 'Burst plate — section four. If it isn't welded back soon, we'll take worse damage.'

The merchant leaned toward Torres. 'Can you take this rod and reel?' he asked. 'I need a break from it, I feel my judgement getting less quick, and as for the repair, we must often make such in my primitive old days.'

Torres nodded, grim-faced. 'You ought to enjoy this, you know,' van Rijn reproved him, and undid his harness.

Rising, he crossed a deck which pitched beneath his feet almost as if he were in a watercraft. *Gantok* was still making full-powered spurts of drive, trying to stress *Mercury* into ruin. She might succeed yet. The hole in the side had sealed itself, but remained a point of weakness from which further destruction could spread.

At the lockers, van Rijn clambered into his outsize spacesuit. Hadn't worn armor in a long time . . . forgotten how quickly sweat made it stink . . . The equipment he would need was racked nearby. He loaded it onto his back and cycled through the airlock. Emerging on the hull, he was surrounded by a darkness-whitening starblaze.

Any of those shocks that rolled and yawed the ship underfoot could prove too much for the grip of his bootsoles upon her. Pitched out beyond the hyperdrive fields and reverting to normal state, he would be forever lost in a microsecond as the craft flashed by at translight hyperspeed. Infinity was a long ways to fall.

Electric discharges wavered blue around him. Occasionally he saw a flash in the direction of *Gantok*, when phasings happened momentarily to coincide. She must be shooting wildly, on the one-in-a-billion chance that some missile would be in exactly the right state when it passed through *Mercury* . . . or through van Rijn's stomach . . . no, through the volume of space where these things coexisted with different frequencies . . . must be precise . . .

There was the fit-for-perdition hull plate. Clamp on the jack, bend the thing back toward some rough semblance of its proper shape . . . ah, heave ho . . . electric-powered hydraulics or not, it still took strength to do this; maybe some muscle remained under the blubber . . . lay out the reinforcing bars, secure them temporarily, unlimber your torch, slap down your glare filter . . . handle a flame and recall past years when he went hell-roaring in his own person . . . whoops, that lunge nearly tossed him off into God's great icebox!

He finished his job, reflected that the next ship of this model would need still heavier bracing, and crept back to the airlock, trying to ignore the aches that throbbed in his entire body. As he came inside, the rolling and plunging and racketing stopped. For an instant he wondered if he had been stricken deaf.

Torres' face, wet and haggard, popped into an intercom screen. Hoarsely, he said: 'They've quit. They must realize their own boat will most likely go to pieces before ours – '

Van Rijn, who had heard him through a sonic pickup in his space helmet, straightened his bruised back and whooped. 'Excellent! Now pull us up quick according to plan, you butterbrain!'

He felt the twisting sensation of reversion to normal state, and the hyperdrive thrum died away. Almost he lost his footing as *Mercury* flew off sidewise.

It had been Rentharik's last, desperate move, killing his oscillations, dropping solidly back into the ordinary condition of things where no speed can be greater than that of light. Had his opponent not done likewise, had the ships drawn apart at such an unnatural rate, stresses along the force-beams linking them would promptly have destroyed both, and he would have had that much vengeance. The Terran craft was, however, equipped with a detector coupled to an automatic cutoff, for just this possibility.

Torres barely averted a collision. At once he shifted *Mercury* around until her beams, unbreakably strong, held her within a few meters of *Gantok*, at a point where the weapons of the latter could not be brought to bear. If the Borthudian crew should be wild enough to suit up and try to cross the intervening small distance, to cut a way in and board, it would be no trick to flick them off into the deeps with a small auxiliary pressor.

Van Rijn bellowed mirth, hastened to discard his gear, and sought the bridge for a heart-to-heart talk with Rentharik. ' – You is now enveloped in our hyperfield any time we switch it on, and it is strong enough to drag you along no matter what you do with your engines, understand? We is got several times your power. You better relax and let us take you with us peaceful, because if we get any suspicions about you, we will use our beams to pluck your vessel in small bits. Like they say on Earth, what is sauce for the stews is sauce for the pander . . . Do not use bad language, please; my receiver is blushing.' To his men: 'Hokay, full speed ahead with this little minnow what thought it was a shark!'

A laser call as they entered the Antarean System brought a League cruiser out to meet them. The colony was worth that much protection against bandits, political agitators, and other imaginable nuisances. Though every planet here was barren, the innermost long since engulfed by the expansion of the great dying sun, sufficient mineral wealth existed on the outer worlds – together with a convenient location as a trade center for this entire sector – to support a human population equal to that of Luna. Van Rijn turned his prize over to the warcraft and let Torres bring the battered *Mercury* in. Himself, he slept a great deal, while Dorcas kept her ears covered. Though the

Borthudians had, sanely, stayed passive, the strain of keeping alert for some further attempt of theirs had been considerable.'

Torres had wanted to communicate with the prisoners, but van Rijn would not allow it. 'No, no, my boy, we unmoralize them worse by refusing the light of our eyes. I want the good Captain Rentharik's fingernails chewed down to the elbow when I see him again.'

Having landed, he invited himself to stay at the governor's mansion in Redsun City and make free use of wine cellar and concubines. Between banquets, he found time to check on local prices and raise the tag on pepper a millicredit per gram. The settlers would grumble, but they could afford it. Besides, were it not for him, their meals would be drab affairs, or else they'd have to synthesize their condiments at twice the cost, so didn't he deserve an honest profit?

After three days of this, he decided it was time to summon Rentharik. He lounged on the governor's throne in the high-pillared reception hall, pipe in right fist, bottle in left, small bells braided into his ringlets but merely a dirty bathrobe across his belly. One girl played on a shiverharp, one fanned him with peacock feathers, and one sat on an arm of the seat, giggling and dropping chilled grapes into his mouth. For the time being, he approved of the universe.

Gaunt and bitter between two League guardsmen, Rentharik advanced across the gleaming floor, halted before his captor, and waited.

'Ah, so. Greetings and salubrications,' van Rijn boomed. 'I trust you have had a pleasant stay? The local jails are much recommended, I am told.'

'For your race, perhaps,' the Borthudian said in dull anger. 'My crew and I have been wretched.'

'Dear me. My nose bleeds for you.'

Pride spat: 'More will bleed erelong, you pirate. His Mightiness will take measures.'

'Your maggoty kinglet will take no measurements except of how far his crest is fallen,' declared van Rijn. 'If the civilized planets did not dare fight when he was playing buccaneer, he will not when the foot is in the other shoe. No, he will accept the facts and learn to love them.'

99

'What are your immediate intentions?' Rentharik asked stoically.

Van Rijn stroked his goatee. 'Well, now it may be we can collect a little ransom, perhaps, eh? If not, the local mines are always short of labor, because conditions is kind of hard. Criminals get assigned to them. However, out of my sugar-sweet goodness, I let you choose one person, not yourself, what may go home freely and report what has happened. I will supply a boat what can make the trip. After that we negotiate, starting with rental on the boat.'

Rentharik narrowed his eyes. 'See here. I know how your vile mercantile society works. You do nothing that has no money return. You are not capable of it. And to equip a vessel like yours – able to seize a warship – must cost more than the vessel can ever hope to earn.'

'Oh, very quite. It costs about three times as much. Of course, we gain some of that back from auctioning off our prizes, but I fear they is too specialized to raise high bids.'

'So. We will strangle your Antares route. Do not imagine we will stop patrolling our sovereign realm. If you wish a struggle of attrition, we can outlast you.'

'Ah, ah.' Van Rijn waggled his pipestem. 'That is what you cannot do, my friend. You can reduce our gains considerably, but you cannot eliminate them. Therefore we can continue our traffic so long as we choose. You see, each voyage nets an average thirty percent profit.'

'But it costs three hundred percent of that profit to outfit a ship –'

'Indeed. But we are only special-equipping every *fourth* ship. That means we operate on a small margin, yes, but a little arithmetic should show you we can still scrape by in the black ink.'

'Every fourth?' Rentharik shook his head, frankly puzzled. 'What is your advantage? Out of every four encounters, we will win three.'

'True. And by those three victories, you capture twelve slaves. The fourth time, we rope in twenty Borthudian spacemen. The loss of ships we can absorb, because it will not go on too long and will be repaid us. You see, you will never know beforehand

100

which craft is going to be the one that can fight back. You will either have to disband your press gangs or quickly get them whittled away.' Van Rijn swigged from his bottle. 'Understand? You is up against loaded dice which will prong you edgewise unless you drop out of the game fast.'

Rentharik crouched, as if to leap, and raged. 'I learned, here, that your spacefolk will no longer travel through the Kossaluth. Do you think reducing the number of impressments by a quarter will change that resolution?'

Van Rijn demonstrated what it is to grin fatly. 'If I know my spacefolk . . . why, of course. Because if you do continue to raid us, you will soon reduce yourselves to such few crews as you are helpless. Then you will *have* to deal with us, or else the League comes in and overthrows your whole silly hermit-kingdom system. That would be so quick and easy an operation, there would be no chance for the politicians at home to interfere.

'Our terms will include freeing of all slaves and big fat indemnities. Great big fat indemnities. They do right now, naturally, so the more prisoners you take in future, the worse it will cost you. Any man or woman worth salt can stand a couple years' service on your nasty rustbuckets, if this means afterward getting paid enough to retire on in luxuriance. Our main trouble will be fighting off the excessive volunteers.'

He cleared his throat, buttered his tone, and went on: 'Is you therefore not wise for making agreement right away? We will be very lenient if you do. Since you are then short of crews, you can send students to our academies at not much more than the usual fees. Otherwise we will just want a few minor trade concessions – '

'And in a hundred years, you will own us,' Rentharik half-snarled, half-groaned.

'If you do not agree, by damn, we will own you in much less time than that. You can try impressing more of our people and bleed yourselves to death; then we come in and free them and take what is left of everything you had. Or you can leave our ships alone on their voyages – but then your subjects will soon know, and your jelly-built empire will break up nearly as quick, because how you going to keep us from delivering subversionists and weapons for rebels along the way? Or you can return your slaves right off, and make the kind of bargain with us what I have been pumping at you. In that case, you at least arrange that your ruling class loses power only, in an orderly way, and not their lives. Take your choice. You is well enough hooked that it makes no big matter to me.'

The merchant shrugged. 'You, personal,' he continued, 'you pick your delegate and we will let him go report to your chief swine. You might maybe pass on the word how Nicholas van Rijn of the Polestechnic League does nothing without good reason, nor says anything what is not calm and sensible. Why, just the name of my ship could have warned you.'

Rentharik seemed to shrivel. 'How?' he whispered.

'Mercury,' the man explained, 'was the old Roman god of commerce, gambling . . . and, *ja*, thieves.'

The following tale is here because it shows a little more of the philosophy and practice which once animated the Polesotechnic League. Grip well: already these were becoming somewhat archaic, if not obsolete. Nevertheless, the person concerned appears to have soared high for long years afterward. Children of his moved to Avalon with Falkayn. This story was written in her later years by one of them, Judith, drawing upon her father's reminiscences when she was young and on a good knowledge of conditions as they had been in his own youth. It appeared in a periodical of the time called *Morgana*.

ESAU

The cab obtained clearance from certain machines and landed on the roof of the Winged Cross. Emil Dalmady paid and stepped out. When it took off, he felt suddenly very alone. The garden was fragrant around him in a warm deep-blue summer's dusk; at this height, the sounds of Chicago Integrate were a murmur as of a distant ocean; the other towers and the sky-ways between them were an elven forest through which flitted will-o'-the-wisp aircars and beneath which – as if Earth had gone transparent – a fantastic galaxy of many-colored lights was blinking awake farther than eye could reach. But the penthouse bulking ahead might have been a hill where a grizzly bear had its den.

The man squared his shoulders. *Haul in*, he told himself. *He won't eat you.* Anger lifted afresh. *I might just eat him.* He strode forward: a stocky, muscular figure in a blue zipskin, features broad, high of cheekbones, snubnosed, eyes green and slightly tilted, hair reddish black.

But despite stiffened will, the fact remained that he had not expected a personal interview with any merchant prince of the Polesotechnic League, and in one of the latter's own homes. When a live butler had admitted him, and he had crossed an improbably long stretch of trollcat rug to the VieWall end of a luxury-cluttered living room, and was confronting Nicholas van Rijn, his throat tightened and his palms grew wet.

'Good evening,' the host rumbled. 'Welcome.' His corpulent corpus did not rise from the lounger. Dalmady didn't mind. Not only bulk but height would have dwarfed him. Van Rijn waved a hand at a facing seat; the other gripped a liter tankard of beer. 'Sit. Relax. You look quivery like a blanc-mange before a firing squad. What you drink, smoke, chew, sniff, or elsewise make amusements with?'

Dalmady lowered himself to an edge. Van Rijn's great hook-beaked, multichinned, mustached and goateed visage, framed in black shoulder-length ringlets, crinkled with a grin. Beneath the sloping brow, small jet eyes glittered at the newcomer. 'Relax,' he urged again. 'Give the form-fitting a chance. Not so fun-making an embrace like a pretty girl, but less extracting, ha? I think maybe a little glass Genever and bitters over dry ice is a tranquilizator for you.' He clapped.

'Sir,' Dalmandy said, harshly in his tension, 'I don't want to seem ungracious, but – '

'But you came to Earth breathing flame and brimrocks, and went through six echelons of the toughest no-saying secretaries and officers what the Solar Spice and Liquors Company has got, like a bulldozer chasing a cowdozer, demanding to see whoever the crockhead was what fired you after what you done yonder-ways. Nobody had a chance to explain. Trouble was, they assumptioned you knew things what they take for granted. So natural, what they said sounded to you like a flushoff and you hurricaned your way from them to somebody else.'

Van Rijn offered a cigar out of a gold humidor whose work-manship Dalmady couldn't identify except that it was non-human. The young man shook his head. The merchant selected one himself, bit off the end and spat that expertly into a receptor, and inhaled the tobacco to ignition. 'Well,' he continued, 'somebody would have got through into you at last, only then I learned about you and ordered this meeting. I would have wanted to talk at you anyhows. Now I shall clarify everything like Hindu butter.'

His geniality was well nigh as overwhelming as his wrath would have been, assuming the legends about him were true. *And he could be setting me up for a thunderbolt*, Dalmady thought, and clung to his indignation as he answered:

'Sir, if your outfit is dissatisfied with my conduct on Saleiman, it might at least have told me why, rather than sending a curt message that I was being replaced and should report to HQ.

Unless you can prove to me that I bungled, I will not accept demotion. It's a question of personal honor more than professional standing. They think that way where I come from. I'll quit. And . . . there are plenty of other companies in the League that will be glad to hire me.'

'True, true, in spite of every candle I burn to St Dismas.' Van Rijn sighed through his cigar, engulfing Dalmady in smoke. 'Always they try to pirate my executives what have not yet sworn fealty, like the thieves they are. And I, poor old lonely fat man, trying to run this enterprise personal what stretches across so many whole worlds, even with modern computer technology I get melted down from overwork, and too few men for helpers what is not total gruntbrains, and some of them got to be occupied just luring good executives away from elsewhere.' He took a noisy gulp of beer. 'Well.'

'I suppose you've read my report, sir,' was Dalmady's gambit.

'Today. So much information flowing from across the light-years, how can this weary old noggle hold it without data flowing back out like ear wax? Let me review to make sure I got it tesseract. Which means – ho, ho! – straight in four dimensions.'

Van Rijn wallowed deeper into his lounger, bridged hairy fingers, and closed his eyes. The butler appeared with a coldly steaming and hissing goblet. *If this is his idea of a small drink— !* Dalmady thought. Grimly, he forced himself to sit at ease and sip.

'Now.' The cigar waggled in time to the words. 'This star what its discoverer called Osman is out past Antares, on the far edge of present-day regular-basis League activities. One planet is inhabited, called by humans Suleiman. Sobjovian; life based on hydrogen, ammonia, methane; primitive natives, but friendly. Turned out, on the biggest continent grows a plant we call . . . um-m-m . . . bluejack, what the natives use for a spice and tonic. Analysis showed a complicated blend of chemicals, answering sort of to hormonal stuffs for us, with synergistic efforts. No good to oxygen breathers, but maybe we can sell to hydrogen breathers elsewhere.

'Well, we found very few markets, at least what had anythings to offer we wanted. You need a special biochemistry for bluejack to be beneficial. So synthesis would cost us more, counting investment and freight charges from chemical-lab centers, than direct harvesting by natives on Suleiman, paid for in trade goods. Given that, we could show a wee profit. Quite teensy – whole operation is near-as-damn marginal – but as long as things stayed peaceful, well, why not turn a few honest credits?

'And things was peaceful, too, for years. Natives cooperated fine, bringing in bluejack to warehouses. Outshipping was one of those milk runs where we don't knot up capital in our own vessels, we contract with a freighter line to make regular calls. Oh, *ja*, contretemps kept on countertiming – bad seasons, bandits raiding caravans, kings getting too greedy about taxes – usual stuffing, what any competent factor could handle on the spot, so no reports about it ever come to pester me.

'And then – Ahmed, more beer! – real trouble. Best market for bluejack is on a planet we call Babur. Its star, Mogul, lies in the same general region, about thirty light-years from Osman. Its top country been dealing with Technic civilization off and on for decades. Trying to modernize, they was mainly interested in robotics for some reason; but at last they did pile together enough outplanet exchange for they could commission a few hyperdrive ships built and crews trained. So now the Solar Commonwealth and other powers got to treat them with a little more respect; blast cannon and nuclear missiles sure improve manners, by damn! They is still small tomatoes, but ambitious. And to them, with the big domestic demand, bluejack is not an incidental thing.'

Van Rijn leaned forward, wrinkling the embroidered robe that circled his paunch. 'You wonder why I tell you what you know, ha?' he said. 'When I need direct reports on a situation, especial from a world as scarcely known as Suleiman, I can't study each report from decades. Data retrieval got to make me an abstract. I check with you now, who was spotted there, whether the machine give me all what is significant to our talking. Has I been correct so far?'

'Yes,' Dalmady said. 'But –'

* * *

Yvonne Vaillancourt looked up from a console as the factor passed the open door of her collation lab. 'What's wrong, Emil?' she asked. 'I heard you clattering the whole way down the hall.'

Dalmady stopped for a look. Clothing was usually at a minimum in the Earth-conditioned compound, but, while he had grown familiar with the skins of its inhabitants, he never tired of hers. Perhaps, he had thought, her blonde shapeliness impressed him the more because he had been born and raised on Altai. The colonists of that chill planet went heavily dressed of necessity. The same need to survive forced austere habits on them; and, isolated in a largely unexplored frontier section, they received scant news about developments in the core civilization.

When you were half a dozen humans on a world whose very air was death to you – when you didn't even have visitors of your own species, because the ship that regularly called belonged to a Cynthian carrier – you had no choice but to live in free and easy style. Dalmady had had that explained to him while he was being trained for this post, and recognized it and went along with it. But he wondered if he would ever become accustomed to the *casualness* of the sophisticates whom he bossed.

'I don't know,' he answered the girl. 'The Thalassocrat wants me at the palace.'

'Why, he knows perfectly well how to make a visi call.'

'Yes, but a nomad's brought word of something nasty in the Uplands, and won't come near the set. Afraid it'll imprison his soul, I imagine.'

'M-m-m, I think not. We're still trying to chart the basic Suleimanite psychology, you know, with only inadequate data from three or four cultures to go on . . . but they don't seem to have animistic tendencies like man's. Ceremony, yes, in abundance, but nothing we can properly identify as magic or religion.'

Dalmady barked a nervous laugh. 'Sometimes I think my whole staff considers our commerce an infernal nuisance that keeps getting in the way of their precious science.'

'Sometimes you'd be right,' Yvonne purred. 'What'd hold us here except the chance to do research?'

'And how long would your research last if the company closed down this base?' he flared. 'Which it will if we start losing money. My job's to see that we don't. I could use co-operation.'

She slipped from her stool, came to him, and kissed him lightly. Her hair smelled like remembered steppe grass warmed by an orange sun, rippling under the rings of Altai. 'Don't we help?' she murmured. 'I'm sorry, dear.'

He bit his lip and stared past her, down the length of gaudy murals whose painting had beguiled much idle time over the years. 'No, I'm sorry,' he said with the stiff honesty of his folk. 'Of course you're all loyal and— It's me. Here I am, the youngest among you, a half-barbarian herdboy, supposed to make a go of things . . . in one of the easiest, most routinized outposts in this sector . . . and after a bare fifteen months – '

If I fail, he thought, *well, I can return home, no doubt, and dismiss the sacrifice my parents made to send me to managerial school offplanet, scorn the luck that Solar Spice and Liquors had on opening here and no more experienced employee to fill it, forget every dream about walking in times to come on new and unknown worlds that really call forth every resource a man has to give. Oh, yes, failure isn't fatal, except in subtler ways than I have words for.*

'You fret too much.' Yvonne patted his cheek. 'Probably this is just another tempest in a chickenhouse. You'll bribe somebody, or arm somebody, or whatever's needful, and that will once again be that.'

'I hope so. But the Thalassocrat acted – well, not being committed to xenological scholarly precision, I'd say he acted worried too.' Dalmady stood a few seconds longer, scowling, before: 'All right, I'd better be on my way.' He gave her a hug. 'Thanks, Yvonne.'

She watched him till he was out of sight, then returned to her work. Officially she was the trade post's secretary-treasurer, but such duties seldom came to her except when a freighter had landed. Otherwise she used the computers to try to find patterns in what fragments of knowledge her colleagues could wrest from a world – an entire, infinitely varied world – and hoped that a few scientists elsewhere might eventually scan a report on Suleiman (one among thousands of planets) and be interested.

Airsuit donned, Dalmady left the compound by its main personnel lock. Wanting time to compose himself, he went afoot through the city to the palace.

If they were city and palace.

He didn't know. Books, tapes, lectures, and neuroinductors had crammed him with information about this part of this continent; but those were the everyday facts and skills needed to manage operations. Long talks with his subordinates here had added a little insight, but only a little. Direct experience with the autochthons was occasionally enlightening, but just as apt to be confusing. No wonder that, once a satisfactory arrangement was made with Coast and Upland tribes (?), his predecessors had not attempted expansion or improvement. When you don't understand a machine but it seems to be running reasonably smoothly, you don't tinker much.

Outside the compound's forcefield, local gravity dragged at him with forty percent greater pull than Earth's. Though his suit was light and his muscles hard, the air recycler necessarily included the extra mass of a unit for dealing with the hydrogen that seeped through any material. Soon he was sweating. Nevertheless it was as if the chill struck past all thermostatic coils, into his heavy bones.

High overhead stood Osman, a furious white spark, twice as luminous as Sol but, at its distance, casting a bare sixteenth of what Earth gets. Clouds, tinged red by organic compounds, drifted on slow winds through a murky sky where one of the three moons was dimly visible. That atmosphere bore thrice a terrestrial standard pressure. It was mostly hydrogen and helium, with vapors of methane and ammonia and traces of other gas. Greenhouse effect did not extend to unfreezing water.

Indeed, the planetary core was overlaid by a shell of ice, mixed with rock, penetrated by tilted metal-poor strata. The land glittered amidst its grayness and scrunched beneath Dalmady's boots. It sloped down to a dark, choppy sea of liquid ammonia whose horizon was too remote – given a 17,000-

kilometer radius – for him to make out through the red-misted air.

Ice also were the buildings that rose blocky around him. They shimmered glasslike where doorways or obscure carved symbols did not break their smoothness. There were no streets in the usual sense, but aerial observation had disclosed an elaborate pattern in the layout of structures, about which the dwellers could not or would not speak. Wind moved ponderously between them. The air turned its sound, every sound, shrill.

Traffic surged. It was mainly pedestrian, natives on their business, carrying the oddly shaped tools and containers of a fireless neolithic nonhuman culture. A few wagons lumbered in with produce from the hinterland; their draught animals suggested miniature dinosaurs modeled by someone who had heard vague rumors of such creatures. A related, more slender species was ridden. Coracles bobbed across the sea; you might as well say the crews were fishing, though a true fish could live here unprotected no longer than a man.

Nothing reached Dalmady's earphones except the wind, the distant wave-rumble, the clop of feet and creak of wagons. Suleimanites did not talk casually. They did communicate, however, and without pause: by gesture, by ripple across erectile fur, by delicate exchanges between scent glands. They avoided coming near the human, but simply because his suit was hot to their touch. He gave and received many signals of greeting. After two years – twenty-five of Earth's Coast and Uplands alike were becoming dependent on metal and plastic and energy-cell trade goods. Local labor had been eagerly available to help build a spaceport on the mesa overlooking town, and still did most of the work. That saved installing automatic machinery – one reason for the modest profit by this station.

Dalmady leaned into his uphill walk. After ten minutes he was at the palace.

The half-score natives posted outside the big, turreted building were not guards. While wars and robberies occurred on Suleiman, the slaying of a 'king' seemed to be literally unthinkable. (An effect of pheromones? In every community the xenologists had observed thus far, the leader ate special foods

111

which his followers insisted would poison anyone else; and maybe the followers were right.) The drums, plumed canes, and less identifiable gear which these beings carried were for ceremonial use.

Dalmady controlled his impatience and watched with a trace of pleasure the ritual of opening doors and conducting him to the royal presence. The Suleimanites were a graceful and handsome species. They were plantigrade bipeds, rather like men although the body was thicker and the average only came to his shoulder. The hands each bore two fingers between two thumbs, and were supplemented by a prehensile tail. The head was round, with a parrotlike beak, tympani for hearing, one large golden hued eye in the middle and two smaller, less developed ones for binocular and peripheral vision. Clothing was generally confined to a kind of sporran, elaborately patterned with symbols, to leave glands and mahogany fur available for signals. The fact that Suleimanite languages had so large a nonvocal component handicapped human efforts at understanding as much as anything else did.

The Thalassocrat addressed Dalmady by voice alone, in the blue-glimmering ice cavern of his audience room. Earphones reduced the upper frequencies to some the man could hear. Nonetheless, that squeak and gibber always rather spoiled the otherwise impressive effect on flower crown and carven staff. So did the dwarfs, hunchbacks, and cripples who squatted on rugs and skin-draped benches. It was not known why household servants were always recruited among the handicapped. Suleimanites had tried to explain when asked, but their meaning never came through.

'Fortune, power, and wisdom to you, Factor.' They didn't use personal names on this world, and seemed unable to grasp the idea of an identification which was not a scent-symbol.

'May they continue to abide with you, Thalassocrat.' The vocalizer on his back transformed Dalmady's version of local speech into sounds that his lips could not bring forth.

'We have here a Master of caravaneers,' the monarch said.

Dalmady went through polite ritual with the Uplander, who was tall and rangy for a Suleimanite, armed with a stone-headed tomahawk and a trade rifle designed for his planet, his barbarianism showing in gaudy jewels and bracelets. They were okay, however, those hill-country nomads. Once a bargain had been struck, they held to it with more literal-mindedness than humans could have managed.

'And what is the trouble for which I am summoned, Master? Has your caravan met bandits on its way to the Coast? I will be glad to equip a force for their suppression.'

Not being used to talking with me, the chief went into full Suleimanite language – his own dialect, at that – and became incomprehensible. One of the midgets stumped forward. Dalmady recognized him. A bright mind dwelt in that poor little body, drank deep of whatever knowledge about the universe was offered, and in return had frequently helped with counsel or knowledge. 'Let me ask him out, Factor and Thalassocrat,' he suggested.

'If you will, Advisor,' his overlord agreed.

'I will be in your debt, Translator,' Dalmady said, with his best imitation of the prancing thanks-gesture.

Beneath the courtesies, his mind whirred and he found himself holding his breath while he waited. Surely the news couldn't be really catastrophic!

He reviewed the facts, as if hoping for some hitherto unnoticed salvation in them. With the little axial tilt, Suleiman lacked seasons. Bluejack needed the cool, dry climate of the Uplands, but there it grew the year around. Primitive natives, hunters and gatherers, picked it in the course of their wanderings. Every several months, terrestrial, such a tribe would make rendezvous with one of the more advanced nomadic herding communities, who bartered for the parched leaves and fruits. A caravan would then form and make the long trip to this city, where Solar's folk would acquire the bales in exchange for Technic merchandise. You could count on a load arriving about twice a month. Four times in an Earth-side year, the Cynthian vessel took away the contents of Solar's warehouse ... and left a far more precious cargo of letters, tapes, journals, books, news from the stars that were so rarely seen in these gloomy heavens.

It wasn't the most efficient system imaginable, but it was the cheapest, once you calculated what the cost would be – in capital investment and civilized-labor salaries – of starting plantations. And costs must be kept low or the enterprise would change from a minor asset to a liability, which would soon be liquidated. As matters were, Suleiman was a typical outpost of its kind: to the scientists, a fascinating study and a chance to win reputation in their fields; to the factors, a comparatively easy job, a first step on a ladder at the top of which waited the big, glamorous, gorgeously paid managerial assignments.

Or thus it had been until now.

The Translator turned to Dalmady. 'The Master says this,' he piped. 'Lately in the Uplands have come what he calls – no, I do not believe that can be said in words alone – It is clear to me, they are machines that move about harvesting the blue-jack.'

'What?' The man realized he had exclaimed in Anglic. Through suddenly loud pulses, he heard the Translator go on:

'The wild folk were terrified and fled those parts. The machines came and took what they had stored against their next rendezvous. That angered this Master's nomads, who deal there. They rode to protest. From afar they saw a vessel, like the great flying vessel that lands here, and a structure a-building. Those who oversaw that work were . . . low, with many legs and claws for hands . . . long noses . . . A gathering robot came and shot lightning past the nomads. They saw they too must flee, lest its warning shot become deadly. The Master himself took a string of remounts and posted hither as swiftly as might be. In words, I cannot say more of what he has to tell.'

Dalmady gasped into the frigid blueness that enclosed him. His mouth felt dry, his knees weak, his stomach in upheaval. 'Baburites,' he mumbled. 'Got to be. But why're they doing this to us?'

Brush, herbage, leaves on the infrequent trees, were many shades of black. Here and there a patch of red or brown or blue flowering relieved it, or an ammonia river cataracting down the hills. Further off, a range of ice mountains flashed blindingly; Suleiman's twelve-hour day was drawing to a close, and Osman's rays struck level through a break in roiling ruddy

114

cloud cover. Elsewhere a storm lifted like a dark wall on which lightning scribbled. The dense air brought its thunder-noise to Dalmady as a high drumroll. He paid scant attention. The gusts that hooted around his car, the air pockets into which it lurched, made piloting a fulltime job. A cybernated vehicle would have been too expensive for this niggardly rewarding planet.

'There!' cried the Master. He squatted with the Translator in an after compartment, which was left under native conditions and possessed an observation dome. In deference to his superstitions, or whatever they were, only the audio part of the intercom was turned on.

'Indeed,' the Translator said more calmly. 'I descry it now. Somewhat to our right, Factor – in a valley by a lake – do you see?'

'A moment.' Dalmady locked the altitude controls. The car would bounce around till his teeth rattled, but the grav field wouldn't let it crash. He leaned forward in his harness, tried to ignore the brutal pull on him, and adjusted the scanner screen. His race had not evolved to see at those wavelengths which penetrated this atmosphere best; and the distance was considerable, as distances tend to be on a subjovian.

Converting light frequencies, amplifying, magnifying, the screen flung a picture at him. Tall above shrubs and turbulent ammonia stood a spaceship. He identified it as a Holbert-X freighter, a type commonly sold to hydrogen breathers. There had doubtless been some modifications to suit its particular home world, but he saw none except a gun turret and a couple of missile tube housings.

A prefabricated steel and ferrocrete building was being assembled nearby. The construction robots must be working fast, without pause; the cube was already more than half-finished. Dalmady glimpsed flares of energy torches, like tiny blue novas. He couldn't make out individual shapes, and didn't want to risk coming near enough.

'You see?' he asked the image of Peter Thorson, and transmitted the picture to another screen.

Back at the base, his engineer's massive head nodded. Behind could be seen the four remaining humans. They looked as strained and anxious as Dalmady felt, Yvonne perhaps more so.

'Yeh. Not much we can do about it,' Thorson declared. 'They pack bigger weapons than us. And see, in the corners of the barn, those bays? That's for blast cannon, I swear. Add a heavy-duty forcefield generator for passive defense, and it's a nut we can't hope to crack.'

'The home office –'

'Yeh, they *might* elect to resent the invasion and dispatch a regular warcraft or three. But I don't believe it. Wouldn't pay, in economic terms. And it'd make every kind of hooraw, because remember, SSL hasn't got any legal monopoly here.' Thorson shrugged. 'My guess is, Old Nick'll simply close down on Suleiman, probably wangling a deal with the Baburites that'll cut his losses and figuring to diddle them good at a later date.' He was a veteran mercantile professional, accustomed to occasional setbacks, indifferent to the scientific puzzles around him.

Yvonne, who was not, cried softly, 'Oh, no! We can't! The insights we're gaining –'

And Dalmady, who could not afford a defeat this early in his career, clenched one fist and snapped, 'We can at least talk to those bastards, can't we? I'll try to raise them. Stand by.' He switched the outercom to a universal band and set the Come In going. The last thing he had seen from the compound was her stricken eyes.

The Translator inquired from aft: 'Do you know who the strangers are and what they intend, Factor?'

'I have no doubt they come from Babur, as we call it,' the man replied absently. 'That is a world' – the more enlightened Coast dwellers had acquired some knowledge of astronomy – 'akin to yours. It is larger and warmer, with heavier air. Its folk could not endure this one for long without becoming sick. But they can move about unarmored for a while. They buy most of our bluejack. Evidently they have decided to go to the source.'

'But why, Factor?'

'For profit, I suppose, Translator.' *Maybe just in their non-human cost accounting. That's a giant investment they're making in a medicinal product. But they don't operate under capitalism, under anything that human history ever saw, or so*

116

I've heard. Therefore they may consider it an investment in . . .
empire? No doubt they can expand their foothold here, once
we're out of the way –

The screen came to life.

The being that peered from it stood about waist-high to a man in its erect torso. The rest of the body stretched behind in a vaguely caterpillar shape, on eight stumpy legs. Along that glabrous form was a row of opercula protecting tracheae which, in a dense hydrogen atmosphere, aerated the organism quite efficiently. Two arms ended in claws reminiscent of a lobster's; from the wrists below sprouted short, tough finger-tendrils. The head was dominated by a spongy snout. A Baburite had no mouth. It – individuals changed sex from time to time – chewed food with the claws and put it in a digestive pouch to be dissolved before the snout sucked it up. The eyes were four, and tiny. Speech was by diaphragms on either side of the skull, hearing and smell were associated with the tracheae. The skin was banded orange, blue, white, and black. Most of it was hidden by a gauzy robe.

The creature would have been an absurdity, a biological impossibility, on an Earth-type world. In its own ship, in strong gravity and thick cold air and murk through which shadowy forms moved, it had dignity and power.

It thrummed noises which a vocalizer rendered into fairly good League Latin: 'We expected you. Do not approach closer.'

Dalmady moistened his lips. He felt cruelly young and helpless. 'G-g-greeting. I am the factor.'

The Baburite made no comment.

After a while, Dalmady plowed on: 'We have been told that you . . . well, you are seizing the bluejack territory. I cannot believe that is correct.'

'It is not, precisely,' said the flat mechanical tone. 'For the nonce, the natives may use these lands as heretofore, except that they will not find much bluejack to harvest. Our robots are too effective. Observe.'

The screen flashed over to a view of a squat, cylindrical machine. Propelled by a simple grav drive, it floated several centimeters off the ground. Its eight arms terminated in sensors, pluckers, trimmers, brush cutters. On its back was welded a large basket. On its top was a maser transceiver and a swivel-mounted blaster.

'It runs off accumulators,' the unseen Baburite stated. 'These need only be recharged once in thirty-odd hours, at the fusion generator we are installing, unless a special energy expenditure occurs . . . like a battle, for instance. High-hovering relay units keep the robots in constant touch with each other and with a central computer, currently in the ship, later to be in the block-house. It controls them all simultaneously, greatly reducing the cost per unit.' With no trace of sardonicism: 'You will understand that such a beamcasting system cannot feasibly be jammed. The computer will be provided with missiles as well as guns and defensive fields. It is programmed to strike back at any attempt to hamper its operations.'

The robot's image disappeared, the being's returned. Dalmady felt faint. 'But that would . . . would be . . . an act of war!' he stuttered.

'No. It would be self-protection, legitimate under the rules of the Polesotechnic League. You may credit us with the intelligence to investigate the social as well as physical state of things before we acted and, indeed, to become an associate member of the League. No one will suffer except your company. That will not displease its competitiors. They have assured our representatives that they can muster enough Council votes to prevent sanctions. It is not as if the loss were very great. Let us recommend to you personally that you seek employment elsewhere.'

Uh-huh . . . after I dropped a planet . . . I might maybe get a job cleaning latrines someplace, went through the back of Dalmady's head. 'No,' he protested, 'what about the autochthons? They're hurting already.'

'When the land has been cleared, bluejack plantations will be established,' the Baburite said. 'Doubtless work can be found for some of the displaced savages, if they are sufficiently docile. Doubtless other resources, ignored by you oxygen breathers, await exploitation. We may in the end breed colonists adapted to Suleiman. But that will be of no concern to the League. We have investigated the practical effect of its prohibition on imperialism by members. Where no one else is interested in a

118

case, a treaty with a native government is considered sufficient, and native governments with helpful attitudes are not hard to set up. Suleiman is such a case. A written-off operation that was never much more than marginal, out on an extreme frontier, is not worth the League's worrying about.'

'The principle – '

'True. We would not provoke war, nor even our own expulsion and a boycott. However, recall that you are not being ordered off this planet. You have simply met a superior competitor, superior by virtue of living closer to the scene, being better suited to the environment, and far more interested in succeeding here. We have the same right to launch ventures as you.'

'What do you mean, "we"?' Dalmady whispered. 'Who are you? What are you? A private company, or – '

'Nominally, we are so organized, though like many other League associates we make no secret of this being *pro forma*,' the Baburite told him. 'Actually, the terms on which our society must deal with the Technic aggregate have little relevance to the terms of its interior structure. Considering the differences – sociological, psychological, biological – between us and you and your close allies, our desire to be free of your civilization poses no real threat to the latter and hence will never provoke any real reaction. At the same time, we will never win the freedom of the stars without the resources of modern technology.

'To industrialize with minimum delay, we must obtain the initial capacity through purchase from the Technic worlds. This requires Technic currency. Thus, while we spend what appears to be a disproportionate amount of effort and goods on this bluejack project, it will result in saving outplanet exchange for more important things.

'We tell you what we tell you in order to make clear, not only your harmlessness to the League as a whole, but our determination. We trust you have taped this discussion. It may prevent your employer from wasting our time and energy in counteracting any foredoomed attempts by him to recoup. While you remain on Suleiman, observe well. When you go back, report faithfully.'

The screen blanked. Dalmady tried for minutes to make the connection again, but got no answer.

Thirty days later, which would have been fifteen of Earth's a conference met in the compound. Around a table, in a room hazed and acrid with smoke, sat the humans. In a full-size screen were the images of the Thalassocrat and the Translator, a three-dimensional realism that seemed to breathe out the cold of the ice chamber where they crouched.

Dalmady ran a hand through his hair. 'I'll summarize,' he told them wearily. The Translator's fur began to move, his voice to make low whistles, as he rendered from the Anglic for his king. 'The reports of our native scouts were waiting for me, recorded by Yvonne, when I returned from my own latest flit a couple of hours ago. Every datum confirms every other.

'We'd hoped, you recall, that the computer would be inadequate to cope with us, once the Baburite ship had left.'

'Why should the live crew depart?' Sanjuro Nakamura asked.

'That's obvious,' Thorson said. 'They may not run their domestic economy the way we run ours, but that doesn't exempt them from the laws of economics. A planet like Babur – actually, a single dominant country on it, or whatever they have – still backward, still poor, has limits on what it can afford. They may enjoy shorter lines of communication than we do, but we, at home, enjoy a lot more productivity. At their present stage, they can't spend what it takes to create and maintain a permanent, live-staffed base like ours. Suleiman isn't too healthy for them, either, you know; and they lack even our small background of accumulated experience. So they've got to automate at first, and just send somebody once in a while to check up and collect the harvest.'

'Besides,' Alice Bergen pointed out, 'the nomads are sworn to us. They wouldn't make a deal with another party. Not that the Baburites could use them profitably anyway. We're sitting in the only suitable depot area, the only one whose people have a culture that makes it easy to train them in service jobs for us. So the Baburites have to operate right on the spot where the bluejack grows. The nomads resent having their caravan trade ended, and would stage guerrilla attacks on live workers.'

120

'Whew!' Nakamura said, with an attempted grin. 'I assure you, my question was only rhetorical. I simply wanted to point out that the opposition would not have left everything in charge of a computer if they weren't confident the setup would function, including holding us at bay. I begin to see why their planners concentrated on developing robotics at the beginning of modernization. No doubt they intend to use machines in quite a few larcenous little undertakings.'

'Have you found out yet how many robots there are?' Isabel da Fonseca asked.

'We estimate a hundred,' Dalmady told her, 'though we can't get an accurate count. They operate fast, you see, covering a huge territory – in fact, the entire territory where bluejack grows thickly enough to be worth gathering – and they're identical in appearance except for the relay hoverers.'

'That must be some computer, to juggle so many at once, over such varying conditions,' Alice remarked. Cybernetics was not her field.

Yvonne shook her head; the gold tresses swirled. 'Nothing extraordinary. We have long-range telephotos, taken during its installation. It's a standard multichannel design, only the electronics modified for ambient conditions. Rudimentary awareness: more isn't required, and would be uneconomic to provide, when its task is basically simple.'

'Can't we outwit it, then?' Alice asked.

Dalmady grimaced. 'What do you think my native helpers and I have been trying to do thereabouts, this past week? It's open country; the relayers detect you coming a huge ways off, and the computer dispatches robots. Not many are needed. If you come too close to the blockhouse, they fire warning blasts. That's terrified the natives. Few of them will approach anywhere near, and in fact the savages are starting to evacuate, which'll present us with a nice bunch of hungry refugees. Not that I blame them. A low-temperature organism cooks easier than you or me. I did push ahead, and was fired on for real. I ran away before my armor should be pierced.'

'What about airborne attack?' Isabel wondered.

Thorson snorted. 'In three rattly cars, with handguns? Those robots fly too, remember. Besides, the centrum has forcefields, blast cannon, missiles. A naval vessel would have trouble reducing it.'

'Furthermore,' interjected the Thalassocrat, 'I am told of a threat to destroy this town by airborne weapons, should a serious assault be made on yonder place. That cannot be risked. Sooner would I order you to depart for aye, and strike what bargain I was able with your enemies.'

He can make that stick, Dalmady thought, *by the simple process of telling our native workers to quit.*

Not that that would necessarily make any difference. He recalled the last statement of a nomad Master, as the retreat from a reconnaisance took place, Suleimanites on their animals, man on a gravscooter. 'We have abided by our alliance with you, but you not by yours with us. Your predecessors swore we should have protection from skyborne invaders. If you fail to drive off these, how shall we trust you?' Dalmady had pleaded for time and had grudgingly been granted it, since the cara-vaneers did value their trade with him. *But if we don't solve this problem soon, I doubt the system can ever be renewed.*

'We shall not imperil you,' he promised the Thalassocrat.

'How real is the threat?' Nakamura asked. 'The League wouldn't take kindly to slaughter of harmless autochthons.'

'But the League would not necessarily do more than com-plain,' Thornson said, 'especially if the Baburites argue that we forced them into it. They're banking on its indifference, and I suspect their judgment is shrewd.'

'Right or wrong,' Alice said, 'their assessment of the psycho-politics will condition what they themselves do. And what assessment have they made? What do we know about their ways of thinking?'

'More than you might suppose,' Yvonne replied. 'After all, they've been in contact for generations, and you don't negotiate commercial agreements without having done some studies in depth first. The reason you've not seen much of me, these past days, is that I've buried myself in our files. We possess, right here, a bucketful of information about Babur.'

Dalmady straightened in his chair. His pulse picked up the least bit. It was no surprise that a large and varied xenological library existed in this insignificant outback base. Microtapes were cheaply reproduced, and you never knew who might chance by or what might happen, so you were routinely supplied with references for your entire sector. 'What do we have?' he barked.

Yvonne smiled wryly. 'Nothing spectacular, I'm afraid. The usual: three or four of the principal languages, sketches of history and important contemporary cultures, state-of-technology analyses, statistics on stuff like population and productivity – besides the planetology, biology, psychoprofiling, et cetera. I tried and tried to find a weak point, but couldn't. Oh, I can show that this operation must be straining their resources, and will have to be abandoned if it doesn't quickly pay off. But that's been just as true of us.'

Thorson fumed on his pipe. 'If we could fix a gadget – We have a reasonably well-equipped workshop. That's where I've been sweating, myself.'

'What had you in mind?' Dalmady inquired. The dullness of the engineer's voice was echoed in his own.

'Well, at first I wondered about a robot to go out and hunt theirs down. I could build one, a single one, more heavily armed and armored.' Thorson's hand flopped empty, palm up, on the table. 'But the computer has a hundred; and it's more sophisticated by orders of magnitude than any brain I could cobble together from spare cybernetic parts; and as the Thalassocrat says, we can't risk a missile dropped on our spaceport in retaliation, because it'd take out most of the city.

'Afterward I thought about jamming, or about somehow lousing the computer itself, but that's totally hopeless. It'd never let you get near.'

He sighed. 'My friends, let's admit that we've had the course, and plan how to leave with minimum loss.'

The Thalassocrat stayed imperturbable, as became a monarch. But the Translator's main eye filmed over, his tiny body shrank into itself, and he cried: 'We had hoped – one year our descendants, learning from you, joining you among the uncounted suns – Is there instead to be endless rule by aliens?'

Dalmady and Yvonne exchanged looks. Their hands clasped. He believed the same thought must be twisting in her: *We, being of the League, cannot pretend to altruism. But we are*

123

not monsters either. Some cold accountant in an office on Earth may order our departure. But can we who have been here, who like these people and were trusted by them, can we abandon them and continue to live with ourselves? Would we not forever feel that any blessings given us were stolen?

And the old, old legend crashed into his awareness.

He sat for a minute or two, unconscious of the talk that growled and groaned around him. Yvonne first noticed the blankness in his gaze. 'Emil,' she murmured, 'are you well?'

Dalmady sprang to his feet with a whoop.

'What in space?' Nakamura said.

The Factor controlled himself. He trembled, and small chills ran back and forth along his nerves; but his words came steady. 'I have an idea.'

Above the robes that billowed around him in the wind, the Translator carried an inconspicuous miniature audiovisual two-way. Dalmady in the car which he had landed behind a hill some distance off, Thorson in the car which hovered to relay, Yvonne and Alice and Isabel and Nakamura and the Thalasso-crat in the city, observed a bobbing, swaying landscape on their tuned-in screens. Black leaves streamed, long and ragged, on bushes whose twigs clicked an answer to the whining air; boulders and ice chunks hunched among them; an ammonia fall boomed on the right, casting spray across the field of view. The men in the cars could likewise feel the planet's traction and the shudder of hulls under that slow, thick wind.

'I still think we should've waited for outside help,' Thorson declared on a separate screen. 'That rig's a godawful lash-up.'

'And I still say,' Dalmady retorted, 'your job's made you needlessly fussy in this particular case. Besides, the natives couldn't've been stalled much longer.' *Furthermore, if we can rout the Baburites with nothing but what was on hand, that ought to shine in my record. I'd like to think that's less important to me, but I can't deny it's real.*

One way or another, the decision had to be mine. I am the Factor.

It's a lonesome feeling. I wish Yvonne were here beside me.

'Quiet,' he ordered. 'Something's about to happen.'

124

The Translator had crossed a ridge and was gravscooting down the opposite slope. He required no help at that; a few days of instruction had made him a very fair driver, even in costume. He was entering the robot-held area, and already a skyborne unit slanted to intercept him. In the keen Osmanlight, against ocherous clouds, it gleamed like fire.

Dalmady crouched in his seat. He was airsuited. If his friend got into trouble, he'd slap down his faceplate, open the cockpit, and swoop to an attempted rescue. A blaster lay knobby in his lap. The thought he might come too late made a taste of sickness in his mouth.

The robot paused at hover, arms extended, weapon pointed. The Translator continued to glide at a steady rate. When near collision, the two-way spoke for him: 'Stand aside. We are instituting a change of program.'

Spoke, to the listening computer, in the principal language of Babur.

Yvonne had worked out the plausible phrases, and spent patient hours with vocalizer and recorder until they seemed right. Engineer Thorson, xenologists Nakamura and Alice Bergen, artistically inclined biologist Isabel de Fonseca, Dalmady himself and several Suleimanite advisors who had spied on the Baburites, had created the disguise. Largely muffled in cloth, it didn't have to be too elaborate – a torso shaven and painted; a simple mechanical caterpillar body behind, steered by the hidden tail, automatically pacing its six legs with the wearer's two; a flexible mask with piezoelectric controls guided by the facial muscles beneath; claws and tendrils built over the natural arms, fake feet over the pair of real ones.

A human or an ordinary Suleimite could not successfully have worn such an outfit. If nothing else, they were too big. But presumably it had not occurred to the Baburites to allow for midges existing on this planet. The disguise was far from perfect; but presumably the computer was not programmed to check for any such contingency; furthermore, an intelligent, well-rehearsed actor, adapting his role moment by moment as no robot ever can, creates a gestalt transcending any minor errors of detail.

And . . . logically, the computer *must* be programmed to

allow Baburites into its presence, to service it and collect the bluejack stored nearby.

Nonetheless, Dalmady's jaws ached from the tension on them.

The robot shifted out of the viewfield. In the receiving screens, ground continued to glide away underneath the scooter.

Dalmady switched off audio transmssiion from base. Though none save Yvonne, alone in a special room, was now sending to the Translator, and she via a bone conduction receiver – still, the cheers that had filled the car struck him as premature.

But the kilometers passed and passed. And the blockhouse hove in view, dark, cubical, bristling with sensors and antennae, cornered with the sinister shapes of gun emplacements and missile silos. No forcefield went up. Yvonne said through the Translator's unit: 'Open; do not close again until told,' and the idiot-savant computer directed a massive gate to swing wide.

What happened beyond was likewise Yvonne's job. She scanned through the portal by the two-way, summoned what she had learned of Baburite automation technology, and directed the Translator. Afterward she said it hadn't been difficult except for poor visibility; the builders had used standard layouts and programming languages. But to the Factor it was an hour of sweating, cursing, pushing fingers and belly muscles against each other, staring and staring at the image of enigmatic units which loomed between blank walls, under bluish light that was at once harsh and wan.

When the Translator emerged and the gate closed behind him, Dalmady almost collapsed.

Afterward, though – well, League people were pretty good at throwing a celebration!

* * *

'Yes,' Dalmady said. 'But –'

'Butter me no buts,' van Rijn said. 'Fact is, you reset that expensive computer so it should make those expensive robots stand idle. Why not leastwise use them for Solar?'

'That would have ruined relations with the natives, sir. Primitives don't take blandly to the notion of technological unemployment. So scientific studies would have become impossible. How then would you attract personnel?'

'What personnel would we need?'

'Some on the spot, constantly. Otherwise the Baburites, close as they are, could come back and, for example, organize and arm justly disgruntled Suleimanites against us. Robots or no, we'd soon find the bluejack costing us more than it earned us ... Besides, machines wear out and it costs to replace them. Live native help will reproduce for nothing.'

'Well, you got that much sense, anyhow,' van Rijn rumbled. 'But why did you tell the computer it and its robots should attack *any* kind of machine, like a car or spacecraft, what comes near, and anybody of any shape what tells it to let him in? Supposing situations change, our people can't do nothings with it now neither.'

'I told you, they don't need to,' Dalmady rasped. 'We get along – not dazzlingly, but we get along, we show a profit – with our traditional arrangements. As long as we maintain those, we exclude the Baburites from them. If we ourselves had access to the computer, we'd have to mount an expensive guard over it. Otherwise the Baburites could probably pull a similar trick on us, right? As is, the system interdicts any attempt to modernize operations in the bluejack area. Which is to say, it protects our monopoly – free – and will protect it for years to come.'

He started to rise. 'Sir,' he continued bitterly, 'the whole thing strikes me as involving the most elementary economic calculations. Maybe you have something subtler in mind, but if you do –'

'Whoa!' van Rijn boomed. 'Squat yourself. Reel in some more of your drink, boy, and listen at me. Old and fat I am, but lungs and tongue I got. Also in working order is two other organs, one what don't concern you but one which is my brain, and my brain wants I should get information from you and stuff it.'

Dalmady found he had obeyed.

'You need to see past a narrow specialism,' van Rijn said. 'Sometimes a man is too stupid good at his one job. He booms it, no matter the consequentials to everything else, and makes trouble for the whole organization he is supposed to serve. Like, you considered how Babur would react?'

'Of course. Freelady Vaillancourt – ' *When will I be with her
again?* – 'and Drs Bergen and Nakamura in particular, did an
exhaustive analysis of materials on hand. As a result, we gave
the computer an additional directive: that it warn any approaching vehicle before opening fire. The conversation I had later,
with the spaceship captain or whatever he was, bore out our
prediction.'

(A quivering snout. A black gleam in four minikin eyes. But
the voice, strained through a machine, emotionless: 'Under the
rules your civilization has devised, you have not given us cause
for war; and the League always responds to what it considers
unprovoked attack. Accordingly, we shall not bombard.')

'No doubt they feel their equivalent of fury,' Dalmady said.
'But what can they do? They're realists. Unless they think of
some new stunt, they'll write Suleiman off and try elsewhere.'

'And they buy our bluejack yet?'

'Yes.'

'We should maybe lift the price, like teaching them a lesson
they shouldn't make fumblydiddles with us?'

'You can do that, if you want to make them decide they'd
rather synthesize the stuff. My report recommends against it.'

This time Dalmady did rise. 'Sir,' he declared in anger, 'I may
be a yokel, my professional training may have been in a jerk-
water college, but I'm not a congenital idiot who's mislaid his
pills and I do take my pride seriously. I made the best decision
I was able on Suleiman. You haven't tried to show me where I
went wrong, you've simply had me dismissed from my post, and
tonight you drone about issues that anybody would understand
who's graduated from diapers. Let's not waste more of our
time. Good evening.'

Van Rijn avalanched upward to his own feet. 'Ho, ho!' he
bawled. 'Spirit, too! I like, I like!'

Dumfounded, Dalmady could only gape.

Van Rijn clapped him on the shoulder, nearly felling him,
'Boy,' the merchant said, 'I didn't mean to rub your nose in
nothings except sweet violets. I did have to know, did you
stumble onto your answer, which is beautiful, or can you think
original? Because you take my saying, maybe everybody under-
stands like you what is not wearing diapers no more; but if that

128

is true, why, ninety-nine point nine nine percent of every sophont race is wearing diapers, at least on their brains, and it leaks out of their mouths. I find you is in the oh point oh one percent, and I want you. Hoo-ha, how I want you!'

He thrust the gin-filled goblet back into Dalmady's hand. His tankard clanked against it. 'Drink!'

Dalmady took a sip. Van Rijn began to prowl.

'You is from a frontier planet and so is naive,' the merchant said, 'but that can be outlived like pimples. See, when my underlings at HQ learned you had pulled our nuts from the fire on Suleiman, they sent you a standard message, not realizing an Altaian like you would not know that in such cases the proceeding is SOP,' which he pronounced 'sop'. He waved a gorilla arm, splashing beer on the floor. 'Like I say, we had to check if you was lucky only. If so, we would promote you to be manager someplace better and forget about you. But if you was, actual, extra smart and tough, we don't want you for a manager. You is too rare and precious for that. Would be like using a Hokusai print in a catbox.'

Dalmady raised goblet to mouth, unsteadily. 'What do you mean?' he croaked.

'Entrepreneur! You will keep title of factor, because we can't make jealousies, but what you do is what the old Americans would have called a horse of a different dollar.

'Look.' Van Rijn reclaimed his cigar from the disposal rim, took a puff, and made forensic gestures with it and tankard alike while he continued his earthquake pacing. 'Suleiman was supposed to be a nice routine post, but you told me how little we know on it and how sudden the devil himself came to lunch. Well, what about the real new, real hairy – and real fortune-making – places? Ha?

'You don't want a manager for them, not till they been whipped into shape. A good manager is a very high-powered man, and we need a lot of him. But in his bottom, he is a routineer; his aim is to make things go smooth. No, for the wild places you need an innovator in charge, a man what likes to take risks, a heterodoxy if she is female – somebody what can meet wholly new problems in unholy new ways – you see?

'Only such is rare, I tell you. They command high prices:

high as they can earn for themselves. Natural, I want them earning for me too. So I don't put that kind of factor on salary and dangle a promotion ladder in front of him. No, the entrepreneur kind, first I get his John Bullcock on a ten-year oath of fealty. Next I turn him loose with a stake and my back-up, to do what he wants, on straight commission of ninety percent.

'Too bad nobody typed you before you went in managerial school. Now you must have a while in an entrepreneurial school I got tucked away where nobody notices. Not dull for you; I hear they throw fine orgies; but mainly I think you will enjoy your classes, if you don't mind working till brain-sweat runs out your nose. Afterward you go get rich, if you survive, and have a big ball of fun even if you don't. Hokay?'

Dalmady thought for an instant of Yvonne; and then he thought, *What the deuce, if nothing better develops, in a few years I can set any hiring policies I feel like*; and: 'Hokay!' he exclaimed, and tossed off his drink in a single gulp.

The following story was also written by Judith Dalmady/
Lundgren for the periodical *Morgana*. She based it upon an
incident whereof her father had told her, he having gotten the
tale from one of the persons directly concerned when he was an
entrepreneur in those parts. Hloch includes it, first, because it
shows more than the usual biographies do of a planet on which
Falkayn had, earlier, had a significant adventure. Second, it
gives yet another glimpse into a major human faith, alive unto
this year and surely of influence upon him and his
contemporaries.

THE SEASON OF FORGIVENESS

It was a strange and lonely place for a Christmas celebration –
the chill planet of a red dwarf star, away off in the Pleiades
region, where half a dozen humans laired in the ruins of a city
which had been great five thousand years ago, and everywhere
else reached wilderness.

'No!' said Master Trader Thomas Overbeck. 'We've got too
much work on our hands to go wasting man-hours on a piece of
frivolity.'

'It isn't, sir,' answered his apprentice, Jaun Hernández. 'On
Earth it's important. You have spent your life on the frontier,
so perhaps you don't realize this.'

Overbeck, a large blond man, reddened. 'Seven months here,
straight out of school, and you're telling me how to run my
shop? If you've learned all the practical technique I have to
teach you, why, you may as well go back on the next ship.'

Juan hung his head. 'I'm sorry, sir. I meant no disrespect.'

Standing there, in front of the battered desk, against a
window which framed the stark, sullenly lit landscape and a
snag of ancient wall, he seemed younger than his sixteen Terrestrial years, slight, dark-haired, big-eyed. The company-issue
coverall didn't fit him especially well. But he was quick-witted,
Overbeck realized; he had to be, to graduate from the Academy
that soon. And he was hard-working, afire with eagerness. The
merchants of the League operated over so vast and diverse a
territory that promising recruits were always in short supply.

That practical consideration, as well as a touch of sympathy,
made the chief growl in a milder tone: 'Oh, of course I've no

objection to any small religious observance you or the others may want to hold. But as for doing more—'' He waved his cigar at the scene outside. 'What does it mean, anyway? A date on a chronopiece. A chronopiece adjusted for Earth! Ivanhoe's year is only two-thirds as long; but the globe takes sixty hours to spin around once; and to top it off, this is local summer, even if you don't dare leave the dome unless you're bundled to the ears. You see, Juan, I've got the same right as you to repeat the obvious.'

His laughter boomed loud. While the team kept their living quarters heated, they found it easiest to maintain ambient air pressure, a fourth gain as high as Terrestrial standard. Sound carried strongly. 'Believe it or not,' he finished, 'I do know something about Christmas traditions, including the very old ones. You want to decorate the place and sing "Jingle Bells"? That's how to make 'em ridiculous!'

'Please, no, sir,' Juan said. 'Also on Earth, in the southern hemisphere the feast comes at summer. And nobody is sure what time of year the Nativity really happened.' He knotted his fists before he plunged on. 'I thought not of myself so much, though I do remember how it is in my home. But that ship will come soon. I'm told small children are aboard. Here will be a new environment for them, perhaps frightening at first. Would we not help them feel easy if we welcomed them with a party like this?'

'Hm.' Overbeck sat still a minute, puffing smoke and tugging his chin. His apprentice had a point, he admitted.

Not that he expected the little ones to be anything but a nuisance as far as he himself was concerned. He'd be delighted to leave them behind in a few more months, when his group had ended its task. But part of that task was to set up conditions which would fit the needs of their successors. The sooner those kids adjusted to life here, the sooner the parents could concentrate on their proper business.

And that was vital. Until lately, Ivanhoe had had no more than a supply depot for possible distressed spacecraft. Then a scientific investigation found the *adir* herb in the deserts of another continent. It wouldn't grow outside its own ecology; and it secreted materials which would be valuable starting points for several new organic syntheses. In short, there was money to be gotten. Overbeck's team was assigned to establish a base, make friends with the natives, learn their ways and the ways of their country, and persuade them to harvest the plant in exchange for trade goods.

That seemed fairly well in order now, as nearly as a man could judge amidst foreignness and mystery. The time looked ripe for putting the trade on a regular basis. Humans would not sign a contract to remain for a long stretch unless they could bring their families. Nor would they stay if the families grew unhappy.

And Tom Overbeck wouldn't collect his big, fat bonus until the post had operated successfully for five standard years.

Wherefore the Master Trader shrugged and said, 'Well, okay. If it doesn't interfere too much with work, go ahead.'

He was surprised at how enthusiastically Ram Gupta, Nikolai Sarychev, Mamoru Noguchi, and Philip Feinberg joined Juan's project. They were likewise young, but not boys; and they had no common faith. Yet together they laughed a lot as they made ready. The rooms and passageways of the dome filled with ornaments cut from foil or sheet metal, twisted together from color-coded wire, assembled from painted paper. Smells of baking cookies filled the air. Men went about whistling immemorial tunes.

Overbeck didn't mind that they were cheerful. That was a boost to efficiency, in these grim surroundings. He argued a while when they wanted to decorate outdoors as well, but presently gave in.

After all, he had a great deal else to think about.

A couple of Ivanhoan days after their talk, he was standing in the open when Juan approached him. The apprentice stopped, waited, and listened, for his chief was in conversation with Raffak.

The dome and sheds of the human base looked oddly bright, totally out of place. Behind them, the gray walls of Dahia lifted sheer, ten meters to the parapets, overtopped by bulbous-battlemented watch-towers. They were less crumbled than the buildings within. Today's dwindled population huddled in what

134

parts of the old stone mansions and temples had not collapsed into rubble. A few lords maintained small castles for themselves, a few priests carried on rites behind porticos whose columns were idols, along twisting dusty streets. Near the middle of town rose the former Imperial palace. Quarried for centuries, its remnants were a colossal shapelessness.

The city dwellers were more quiet than humans. Not even vendors in their flimsy booths cried their wares. Most males were clad in leather kilts and weapons, females in zigzag-patterned robes. The wealthy and the military officers rode on beasts which resembled narrow-snouted, feathery-furred horses. The emblems of provinces long lost fluttered from the lances they carried. Wind, shrill in the lanes, bore sounds of feet, hoofs, groaning cartwheels, an occasional call or the whine of a bone flute.

A human found it cold. His breath smoked into the dry air. Smells were harsh in his nostrils. The sky above was deep purple, the sun a dull ruddy disc. Shadows lay thick; and nothing, in that wan light, had the same color as it did on Earth.

The deep tones of his language rolled from Raffak's mouth. 'We have made you welcome, we have given you a place, we have aided you by our labor and counsel,' declared the speaker of the city Elders.

'You have . . . for a generous payment,' Overbeck answered.

'You shall not, in return, exclude Dahia from a full share in the wealth the *adir* will bring.' A four-fingered hand, thumb set oppositely to a man's, gestured outward. Through a cyclopean gateway showed a reach of dusky-green bush, part of the agricultural hinterlad. 'It is more than a wish to better our lot. You have promised us that. But Dahia was the crown of an empire reaching from sea to sea. Though it lies in wreck, we who live here preserve the memories of our mighty ancestors, and faithfully serve their gods. Shall desert-prowling savages wax rich and strong, while we descendants of their overlords remain weak – until they become able to stamp out this final spark of glory? Never!'

'The nomads claim the wild country,' Overbeck said. 'No one has disputed that for many centuries.'

'Dahia disputes it at last. I came to tell you that we have sent forth emissaries to the Black Tents. They bore our demand that Dahia must share in the *adir* harvest.'

Overbeck, and a shocked Juan, regarded the Ivanhoan closely. He seemed bigger, more lionlike than was right. His powerful, long-limbed body would have loomed a full two meters tall did it not slant forward. A tufted tail whipped the bent legs. Mahogany fur turned into a mane around the flat face. lacked a nose – breathing was through slits beneath the jaws – but the eyes glowed green and enormous, ears stood erect, teeth gleamed sharp.

The human leader braced himself, as if against the drag of a gravity slightly stronger than Earth's, and stated: 'You were foolish. Relations between Dahia and the nomads are touchy at best, violent at worst. Let war break out, and there will be no *adir* trade. Then Dahia too will lose.'

'Lose material goods, maybe,' Raffak said. 'Not honor.'

'You have already lost some honor by your action. You knew my people had reached agreement with the nomads. Now you Elders seek to change that agreement before consulting us.' Overbeck made a chopping gesture which signified anger and determination. 'I insist on meeting with your council.'

After an argument, Raffak agreed to this for the next day, and stalked off. Hands jammed into pockets, Overbeck stared after him. 'Well, Juan,' he sighed, 'there's a concrete example for you, of how tricky this business of ours can get.'

'Might the tribes really make trouble, sir?' wondered the boy.

'I hope not.' Overbeck shook his head. 'Though how much do we know, we Earthlings, as short a while as we've been here? Two whole societies, each with its own history, beliefs, laws, customs, desires – in a species that isn't human!'

'What do you suppose will happen?'

'Oh, I'd guess the nomads will refuse flat-out to let the Dahians send gathering parties into their territory. Then I'll have to persuade the Dahians all over again, to let nomads bring the stuff here. That's what happens when you try to make hereditary rivals cooperate.'

'Couldn't we base ourselves in the desert?' Juan asked.

'It's better to have a large labor force we can hire at need, one that stays put,' Overbeck explained. 'Besides, well— ' He looked almost embarrassed. 'We're after a profit, yes, but not to exploit these poor beings. An *adir* trade would benefit Dahia too, both from the taxes levied on it and from developing friendlier relations with the tribesfolk. In time, they could start rebuilding their civilization here. It was great once, before its civil wars and the barbarian invasions that followed.' He paused. 'Don't ever quote me to them.'

'Why not, sir? I should think – '

'*You* should. I doubt they would. Both factions are proud and fierce. They might decide they were being patronized, and resent it in a murderous fashion. Or they might get afraid we intend to undermine their martial virtues, or their religions, or something.' Overbeck smiled rather grimly. 'No, I've worked hard to keep matters simple, on a level where nobody can misunderstand. In native eyes, we Earthlings are tough but fair. We've come to build a trade that will pay off for us, and for no other reason. It's up to them to keep us interested in remaining, which we won't unless they behave. That attitude, that image is clear enough. I hope, for the most alien mind to grasp. They may not love us, but they don't hate us either, and they're willing to do business.'

Juan swallowed and found no words.

'What'd you want of me?' Overbeck inquired.

'Permission to go into the hills, sir,' the apprentice said. 'You know those crystals along Wola Ridge? They'd be beautiful on the Christmas tree.' Ardently: 'I've finished all my jobs for the time being. It will only take some hours, if I can borrow a flitter.'

Overbeck frowned. 'When a fight may be brewing? The Black Tents are somewhere that way, last I heard.'

'You said, sir, you don't look for violence. Besides, none of the Ivanhoans have a grudge against us. And they respect our power. Don't they? Please!'

'I aim to preserve that state of affairs.' Overbeck pondered. 'Well, shouldn't be any risk. And, hm-m-m, a human going out alone might be a pretty good demonstration of confidence . . . Okay,' he decided. 'Pack a blaster. If a situation turns ugly, don't hesitate to use it. Not that I believe you'll get in any

137

scrape, or I wouldn't let you go. But— ' He shrugged. 'There's no such thing as an absolutely safe bet.'

Three hundred kilometers north of Dahia, the wilderness was harsh mountainsides, deep-gashed canyons, umber crags, thinly scattered thorn-shrubs and wind-gnarled trees with ragged leaves. Searching for the mineral which cropped here and there out of the sandy ground, Juan soon lost sight of his flitter. He couldn't get lost from it himself. The aircraft was giving off a radio signal, and the transceiver in his pocket included a directional meter for homing on it. Thus he wandered further than he realized before he had collected a bagful.

However slowly Ivanhoe rotates, its days must end. Juan grew aware of how low the dim red sun was, how long and heavy the shadows. Chilliness had turned to a cold which bit at his bare face. Evening breezes snickered in the brush. Somewhere an animal howled. When he passed a rivulet, he saw that it had begun to freeze.

I'm in no trouble, he thought, *but I am hungry, and late for supper, and the boss will be annoyed.* Even now, it was getting hard for him to see. His vision was meant for bright, yellow-white Sol. He stumbled on rocks. Had his radio compass not been luminous-dialed, he would have needed a flashbeam to read it.

Nevertheless he was happy. The very weirdness of this environment made it fascinating; and he could hope to go on to many other worlds. Meanwhile, the Christmas celebration would be a circle of warmth and cheer, a memory of home – his parents, his brother and two sisters, Tío Pepe and Tía Carmen, the dear small Mexican town and the laughter as children struck at a *piñata* –

'Raielli, Erratan!'

Halt Earthling! Juan jarred to a stop.

He was near the bottom of a ravine, which he was crossing as the most direct way to the flitter. The sun lay hidden behind one wall of it, and dusk filled the heavens. He could just make out boulders and bushes, vague in the gloom.

Then metal caught what light there was in a faint glimmer. He saw spearheads and a single breastplate. The rest of the

138

warriors had only leather harness. They were blurs around him, save where their huge eyes gleamed like their steel.

Juan's heart knocked. *These are friends!* he told himself. *The People of the Black Tents are anxious to deal with us – Then why did they wait here for me? Why have a score of them risen out of hiding to ring me in?*

His mouth felt suddenly parched. He forced it to form words, as well as it could imitate the voice of an Ivanhoan. City and wilderness dwellers spoke essentially the same language. 'G-greeting.' He remembered the desert form of salutation. 'I am Juan Sancho's-child, called Hernández, pledged follower of the merchant Thomas William's-child, called Overbeck, and am come in peace.'

'I am Tokonnen Undassa's-child, chief of the Elassi Clan,' said the lion-being in the cuirass. His tone was a snarl. 'We may no longer believe that any Earthling comes in peace.'

'What?' cried Juan. Horror smote him. 'But we do! How –'

'You camp among the City folk. Now the City demands the right to encroach on our land . . . Hold! I know what you carry.'

Juan had gripped his blaster. The natives growled. Spears drew back, ready to throw. Tokonnen confronted the boy and continued:

'I have heard tell about weapons like yours. A fire-beam, fiercer than the sun, springs forth, and rock turns molten where it strikes. Do you think a male of Elassi fears that?' Scornfully: 'Draw it if you wish.'

Juan did, hardly thinking. He let the energy gun dangle downward in his fingers and exclaimed, 'I only came to gather a few crystals –'

'If you slay me,' Tokonnen warned, 'that will prove otherwise. And you cannot kill more than two or three of us before the spears of the rest have pierced you. We know how feebly your breed sees in the least of shadows.'

'But what do you *want*?'

'When we saw you descend, afar off, we knew what we wanted – you, to hold among us until your fellows abandon Dahia.'

Half of Juan realized that being kept hostage was most likely

139

a death sentence for him. He couldn't eat Ivanhoan food; it was loaded with proteins poisonous to his kind of life. In fact, without a steady supply of antiallergen, he might not keep breathing. How convince a barbarian herder of that?

The other half pleaded, 'You are being wild. What matter if a few City dwellers come out after *adir*? Or . . . you can tell them "no". Can't you? We, we Earthlings – we had nothing to do with the embassy they sent.'

'We dare not suppose you speak truth, you who have come here for gain,' Tokonnen replied. 'What is our freedom to you, if the enemy offers you a fatter bargain? And we remember, yes, across a hundred generations we remember the Empire. So do they in Dahia. They would restore it, cage us within their rule or drive us into the badlands. Their harvesters would be their spies, the first agents of their conquest. This country is ours. It is strong with the bones of our fathers and rich with the flesh of our mothers. It is too holy for an Imperial foot to tread. You would not understand this, merchant.'

'We mean you well,' Juan stammered. 'We'll give you things – '

Tokonnen's mane lifted haughtily against darkling cliff, twilit sky. From his face, unseen in murk, the words rang: 'Do you imagine things matter more to us than our liberty or our land?' Softer: 'Yield me your weapon and come along. Tomorrow we will bring a message to your chief.'

The warriors trod closer.

There went a flash through Juan. He knew what he could do, must do. Raising the blaster, he fired straight upward.

Cloven air boomed. Ozone stung with a smell of thunderstorms. Blue-white and dazzling, the energy beam lanced toward the earliest stars.

The Ivanhoans yelled. By the radiance, Juan saw them lurch back, drop their spears, clap hands to eyes. He himself could not easily look at that lightning bolt. They were the brood of a dark world. Such brilliance blinded them.

Juan gulped a breath and ran.

Up the slope! Talus rattled underfoot. Across the hills beyond! Screams of wrath pursued him.

The sun was now altogether down, and night came on apace.

It was less black than Earth's, for the giant stars of the Pleiades cluster bloomed everywhere aloft, and the nebula which enveloped them glowed lacy across heaven. Yet often Juan fell across an unseen obstacle. His pulse roared, his lungs were aflame.

It seemed forever before he glimpsed his vehicle. Casting a glance behind, he saw what he had feared, the warriors in pursuit. His shot had not permanently damaged their sight. And surely they tracked him with peripheral vision, ready to look entirely away if he tried another flash.

Longer-legged, born to the planet's gravity, they overhauled him, meter after frantic meter. To him they were barely visible, bounding blacknesses which often disappeared into the deeper gloom around. He could not have hoped to pick them all off before one of them got to range, flung a spear from cover, and struck him.

Somehow, through every terror, he marveled at their bravery. *Run, run.*

He had barely enough of a head start. He reeled into the hull, dogged the door shut, and heard missiles clatter on metal. Then for a while he knew nothing.

When awareness came back, he spent a minute giving thanks. Afterward he dragged himself to the pilot chair. *What a scene!* passed across his mind. And, a crazy chuckle: *The old definition of adventure. Somebody else having a hard time a long ways off.*

He slumped into the seat. The vitryl port showed him a sky turned wonderful, a land of dim slopes and sharp ridges – He gasped and sat upright. The Ivanhoans were still outside.

They stood leaning on their useless spears or clinging to the hilts of their useless swords, and waited for whatever he would do. Shakily, he switched on the sound amplifier and bullhorn. His voice boomed over them: 'What do you want?'

Tokonnen's answer remained prideful. 'We wish to know your desire, Earthling. For in you we have met a thing most strange.'

Bewildered, Juan could merely respond with' How so?'

'You rendered us helpless,' Tokonnen said. 'Why did you not at once kill us? Instead, you chose to flee. You must have

141

known we would recover and come after you. Why did you take the unneeded risk?'

'You *were* helpless,' Juan blurted. 'I couldn't have . . . hurt you . . . especially at this time of year.'

Tokonnen showed astonishment. 'Time of year? What has that to do with it?'

'Christmas – ' Juan paused. Strength and clarity of mind were returning to him. 'You don't know about that. It's a season which, well, commemorates one who came to us Earthlings, ages ago, and spoke of peace as well as much else. For us, this is a holy time.' He laid hands on controls. 'No matter. I only ask you believe that we don't mean you any harm. Stand aside. I am about to raise this wagon.'

'No,' Tokonnen said. 'Wait. I ask you, wait.' He was silent for a while, and his warriors with him. 'What you have told us – We must hear further. Talk to us, Earthling.'

Once he had radioed that he was safe, they stopped worrying about Juan at the base. For the next several hours, the men continued their jobs. It was impossible for them to function on a sixty-hour day, and nobody tried. Midnight had not come when they knocked off. Recreation followed. For four of them, this meant preparing their Christmas welcome to the ship.

As they worked outdoors, more and more Dahians gathered, fascinated, to stand silently around the plaza and watch. Overbeck stepped forth to observe the native in his turn. Nothing like this had ever happened before.

A tree had been erected on the flagstones. Its sparse branches and stiff foliage did not suggest an evergreen; but no matter, it glittered with homemade ornaments and lights improvised from electronic parts. Before it stood a manger scene that Juan had constructed. A risen moon, the mighty Pleiades, and the luminous nebular veil cast frost-cold brilliance. The beings who encompassed the square, beneath lean houses and fortress towers, formed a shadow-mass wherein eyes glimmered.

Feinberg and Gupta decorated. Noguchi and Sarychev, who had the best voices, rehearsed. Breath from their song puffed white.

  'O little town of Bethelehem,
  How still we see thee lie –'

142

A muted 'A-a-ahhh!' rose from the Dahians, and Juan landed his flitter.

He bounded forth. Behind him came a native in a steel breast-plate. Overbeck had awaited this since the boy's last call. He gestured to Raffak, speaker of the Elders. Together, human and Ivanhoan advanced to greet human and Ivanhoan.

Tokonnen said, 'It may be we misjudged your intent, City folk. The Earthling tells me we did.'

'And his lord tells me we of Dahia pushed forward too strongly,' Raffak answered. 'That may likewise be.'

Tokonnen touched sword-hilt and warned, 'We shall yield nothing which is sacred to us.'

'Nor we,' said Raffak. 'But surely our two people can reach an agreement. The Earthlings can help us make terms.'

'They should have special wisdom, now in the season of their Prince of Peace.'

'Aye. My fellows and I have begun some hard thinking about that.'

'How do you know of it?'

'We were curious as to why the Earthlings were making beauty, here where we can see it away from the dreadful heat,' Raffak said. 'We asked. In the course of this, they told us some-what of happenings in the desert, which the far-speaker had informed them of.'

'It is indeed something to think about,' Tokonnen nodded. 'They, who believe in peace, are more powerful than us.'

'And it was war which destroyed the Empire. But come,' Raffak invited. 'Tonight be my guest. Tomorrow we will talk.'

They departed. Meanwhile the men clustered around Juan. Overbeck shook his hand again and again. 'You're a genius,' he said. 'I ought to take lessons from you.'

'No, please, sir,' his apprentice protested. 'The thing simply happened.'

'It wouldn't have, if I'd been the one who got caught.'

Sarychev was puzzled. 'I don't quite see what did go on,' he confessed. 'It was good of Juan to run away from those nomads, instead of cutting them down when he had the chance. How-ever, that by itself can't have turned them meek and mild.'

'Oh, no.' Overbeck chuckled. His cigar end waxed and waned

143

like a variable star. 'They're as ornery as ever – same as humans.' Soberly: 'The difference is, they've become willing to listen to us. They can take our ideas seriously, and believe we'll be honest brokers, who can mediate their quarrels.'

'Why could they not before?'

'My fault, I'm afraid. I wasn't allowing for a certain part of Ivanhoan nature. I should have seen. After all, it's part of human nature too.'

'What is?' Gupta asked.

'The need for – ' Overbeck broke off. 'You tell him, Juan. You were the one who did see the truth.'

The boy drew breath. 'Not at first,' he said. 'I only found I could not bring myself kill. Is Christmas not when we should be quickest to forgive our enemies? I told them so. Then . . . when suddenly their whole attitude changed . . . I guessed what the reason must be.' He searched for words. 'They knew – both Dahians and nomads knew – we are strong; we have powers they can't hope to match. That doesn't frighten them. They have to be fearless, to survive in as bleak a country as this.

'Also, they have to be dedicated. To keep going through endless hardship, they must believe in something greater than themselves, like the Imperial dream of Dahia or the freedom of the desert. They're ready to die for those ideals.

'We came, we Earthlings. We offered them a fair, profitable bargain. But nothing else. We seemed to have no other motive than material gain. They could not understand this. It made us too peculiar. They could never really trust us.

'Now that they know we have our own sacrednesses, well, they see we are not so different from them, and they'll heed our advice.'

Juan uttered an unsteady laugh. 'What a long lecture, no?' he ended. 'I'm very tired and hungry. Please, may I go get something to eat and afterward to bed?'

As he crossed the square, the carol followed him:

' – *The hopes and fears of all the years*
Are met in thee tonight.'

THE END